What people are saying about books by *Billy Beasley:*

"Beasley's characters are as natural, intriguing, and as full of life as the Carolina coast they call home. Their conflicts play out in a low country Eden that is as stirring and primal as the passions of its people."

–Joseph McSpadden, Host of the Village Night Owl Podcast and Contributing Editor, *Okra* Magazine.

A Watch Over the Gate

Billy Beasley

REDHAWK
PUBLICATIONS

A WATCH OVER THE GATE
Copyright © 2025 Billy Beasley

ISBN: 978-1-959346-89-0 (Paperback)

Library of Congress Control Number: 2025936144

Cover Design: Erin Mann
Book Design: Erin Mann

Printed in the United States of America.
First printing 2025.

Redhawk Publications
The Catawba Valley Community College Press
2550 Hwy 70 SE
Hickory, NC 28602
https://redhawkpublications.com

To my wife, Julie. This story was her idea.
And to Petra, who I buried on Christmas Eve night, 1994.
She still visits my dreams.

1 ~ Petra

The hill beneath me has grass with thick blades and a softness that feels as if you were resting on pillows. Long ago, after I ambled through the entrance gate, I walked straight to this hill and claimed it as my own. It has proven to be the perfect spot to keep the gate in view. The hill proves only slightly lower than the gate. Between these two peaks is a large valley that is called the East Village. It is one of the many villages, comprised of homes and even mansions that this extravagant place holds.

Several times daily, people and beloved pets make their way through the throngs of cheering people, as they are now. I am always a little disheartened to discover that my master is not part of the coronation. Maybe that is a bit selfish on my part. The roars subsided and Peter closed the brilliant gold gate. I sighed wearily.

There was no darkness, no fear, no hunger, no death, no illness of any kind in this wonderous place, but it will never be the consummate place of residence for me until my master walked through the gate.

David Hill, a minister, and friend of my master, Cole Banks, has assured me frequently that my master will indeed arrive when the time is right. I don't know how he knows, but he seems pretty convinced that we will be reunited.

Occasionally, David ventured up the hill to sit with me as the new people arrived to their forever home. He would perceive my disenchantment that I attempted to conceal, and would rub my head and state firmly, "Petra"—that is my name—but my master called me Pete for the most part. "Cole will be here. I just know it."

Sometimes, I looked at him and speculated as to just how he could be so convinced. "You have no idea how often that his mom and I prayed for him. You will see him again," he would say to me with a smile so warm that it made me feel good all over. "God had his hand on him—

even during the darkest of times. He just did not know it. You will see." He would often add with a slight wink.

Truthfully, I pondered at times if he was trying to convince himself as much as he was trying to reassure me. Perhaps it was a bit of both.

David is such a gentle, humble man, and he has the most comforting voice. Sometimes when he visits, he brings his Chihuahuas. He has a passel of them. I guess when you are a renowned pastor and shepherd—all your pets naturally received the green light right on through the gate of Heaven. I have come to understand in my time here that not every person makes it. In my early days, I asked questions about that and was politely told that those inquiries were not welcome. I guess it makes sense because if you have loved ones that did not make it and you spent time thinking about them—it would not really be Paradise, now would it?

I never cared much for those yappers, as my master referred to them. I am not even certain that yappers is a real word or one he just made up. You would never catch him with a little dog. I remembered when a neighbor was walking some type of four-pound, wire-haired, rodent looking dog along the road in front of our home. He hollered out to the man. I think his name was Sheldon. "Hey, Sheldon. Why don't you get yourself a real dog?" The man tried to offer a retort, but it was hard to come back from that. He just looked down at his dog—sadly shook his head and kept right on walking. He never ventured past our house again.

I know it was not a very nice thing for my master to say and though I could not express it outwardly—I have to tell you that I was about to empty my bladder laughing on the inside.

David told me several times that I could live with his family until my master arrived. Each time, I respectfully declined. I want to be right here watching the gate when he enters. I don't know how long it has been that I have lived on this hill. Time is not exactly a concern here. There is an old joke that I must say I am beyond weary of hearing. Do you have the time one person would ask? It is eternity time the other would bellow out, and they would laugh like they had not heard that worn joke a hundred times.

Please don't get the wrong idea. This place is terrific. You could never imagine a place with such happiness and peace. No one has a bad day here, and there are no rotten kids or people who think that kicking a dog is an okay thing to do. No one goes hungry, and the strange thing is eating is an option but not required, and I don't even pretend to know how God does this, but we don't even have bodily functions.

I hope you do not think of me as a braggart when I tell you that when I lived on the other side, I was a pretty wise dog. Still, my knowledge back there does not hold a candle to the many things I have come to understand during my time residing here in Heaven.

That night that I foolishly wandered off searching for food that I did not need—only to be struck down. I can't recall everything that transpired. One of the many fantastic things about Heaven is that the good memories from back on the other side remain with you, but the less pleasant fade with time. Not that we have time here. You won't find a clock or a watch anywhere. No one ever needs to be in a hurry like they constantly are on the other side.

That is probably what occurred that Christmas Eve night. I saw those headlights from that big truck, and I knew I was in dire trouble. A black dog on a black road was a recipe for disaster. The truck may not have even struck me. It could well have produced a heart attack. And the young lady driving did not even slow down. I guess she was in too big a hurry to be bothered with an ordinary dog like me.

As I drifted upwards, I couldn't recall seeing a mark on my body as it rested on the shoulder of the road off Hinton Avenue in Sea Gate. I never ventured that way until that fateful night. It was the busiest street in our neighborhood. I wish that I would have stuck to my regular route.

Better yet, I should have just stayed at our house on Michelle Drive. My master bought it after the divorce so he could have a home with his son, Cody, but I was a big part of the decision as well.

Cody was a toddler when his parents decided to divorce. It was for the best, as the tension in that house made me want to go outside and get in my barrel filled with hay and be away from the constant quarrels.

I remained at home with Cody and his mom for several months after my master moved out. I wanted to go with him, but he departed so suddenly that all he could find was an apartment that did not allow pets of any kind—even dogs.

They were able to put aside their differences when it came to what was best for me. Cody's mom agreed to allow my master to pick me up every weekday morning, and he took me to work with him. He managed an irrigation company. I stayed in his office most of the day and when he went to check on jobs, he took me with him.

My thoughts granted me more hope that he will be here with me one day. Shoot, now with all of this clarity—I understand completely the conversation that took place with Cody's mom and my master about my moving in with him after they separated. He asked her if he bought a house if he could have me. I remember clearly what he said next. "I need to provide a home for Cody, and Pete is seven years old. I want what is left."

She balked initially at the proposal, and when she did, he offered softly, "You know that dog loves me more."

She relented and graciously offered, "I know that she would be happier with you." She cared greatly about my happiness and let's face facts, as much as I loved my master—I would not have survived the horrid beginning of my life if she would not have spotted me by the dumpsters where someone had discarded me like a bag of trash. I was sick with worms and malnourished, but she brought me home and nursed me until I was well. I will always be grateful for her kindness, but I wanted to dance that day my master picked me up and said as he kissed the top of my broad snout, "Pete, you are going home with me."

Cody and I both loved our new home. I did not understand it at the time, but my master did not. There was a small unoccupied bedroom that only contained unopened boxes. The boxes were packed with books, photos, and sports keepsakes. He chose not to unpack anything beyond what was necessary.

It took me a long time to understand, but I think I have a handle on it now. He bought the house so Cody and I could have a home. He was at a place in his life where he was not going to be happy regardless of where he lived. I do hope that he is content now, though I am not overly optimistic. After all, if I, the most loyal dog in the world could not make him jovial, who possibly could?

Often on desolate nights, we would walk out to the courtyard that he built in this narrow strip of woods behind our home. Cody and I helped, though truthfully, I pretty much just found a spot to lie down and watch until I drifted off to sleep. Cody was only six years old at the time and limited in what he could do. Still, that kid had unbridled energy that was the catalyst that fueled the project to a conclusion.

Many afternoons after my master had worked all day and picked Cody up from school, he was tired and just wanted to relax. Cody would keep asking him on the drive home if they could work on the courtyard. He would sigh and look at the eager look in Cody's eyes and nod his head in agreement. He hated to ever disappoint that child.

That little boy was so cute when his dad would act as if there were no way in the world that he could possibly complete a task without him. He would start the nails and then hold the board in place and let Cody hammer the nail into the wood the remainder of the way. The sheer joy on that child's face that his dad needed his assistance was something to behold. He used both hands to grip the hammer as that was the only way he could garner the strength to complete the task. It was a good thing that I was never asked to help because paws are not conducive to such a chore.

I loved the little boy, but it was not that way from the very beginning. It really concerned me when they first brought him home from the hospital. My initial instinct was to growl, and I rarely growled at anyone—animal or human. Countless little babies, children, and small animals had been in our house, and I loved on them all.

Cody's mom had a soft spot for injured animals, and she was always bringing home a hurt squirrel or bird—you name it. She would gently nurture as many of the animals back to health as she could. I am a little embarrassed to say that I tried to nurse some of them. I didn't realize I had nothing in that regard to offer, but I had compassion for all of them.

I don't know how I knew that Cody was not a stray but a boy that would take precedence over me but I indeed did. My growl really concerned my master. I am lucky I was not banished outside for good, but one cool thing that they did was to allow me to live inside pretty

11

much all the time after Cody came home. They never wanted me to feel like I was less important now that they had a baby.

We lived in Wilmington, North Carolina, a coastal city in the southeastern part of the state. The winters were short and pretty mild most of the time. Before Cody came home, I was an outside dog for most of the warmer months and an inside dog during winter. Even when I was outside, I had a nice fenced-in backyard. There was a barrel for me that was always full of bedding hay that was actually inside a shed. I was doubly protected.

Despite the moderate winters, I did get to play in the snow a few times in my eleven years on earth. It was cold on my paws, but it sure was fun. My master took a picture of me that he proudly displayed on the wall of our home. I was sitting with this sad look etched upon my face—the contrast of the brilliant white snow intertwined in my very black fur. I must confess that while I do look quite pitiful in the photo, I was playing to the camera a bit. I don't think even our masters on earth who love us dearly, understood just how much we actually comprehended. For goodness sakes—dog is God spelled backward. Do you think that was a mistake made by the King of the Universe? That is a rhetorical question, and if you are reading this, I hope you understand that God does not make mistakes. He may not rapidly solve every issue, but that does not mean that he makes errors.

Being such an astute dog, I figured out that while I liked being with my master the most— it pleased him greatly when I loved on Cody. He even taught me a trick. He would say, "Check the baby, Pete." Cody would be sitting or lying on a blanket on the floor, and I would walk over and put my snout right on his chest. My master would just beam. He relaxed once we got past my initial growl that I never repeated. I realized that to not be kind to Cody would hurt my master. That was the last thing I ever desired to do.

Cody was afraid like little boys can be about going to sleep in his bedroom alone at night. I don't know if it was the new house or maybe he just missed his mom. My master would ask me to sit in the room with him until he fell asleep. I was not very good at that particular assignment, especially considering that my master was in the small living room watching television or reading. I loved Cody. Don't get me wrong. But I wanted to be with my master. After a few minutes, I would sneak out of the room, pad quietly down the hall to the living room. Sometimes Cody would hear me leave, and he would call out, "Dad, Pete left me." I would have to go back for a while. I meant no harm to anyone. I just always felt that my place was near my master.

Many of the nights when Cody was with his mom, we ventured out in the night air and walked to the courtyard. I don't think my master cared for nighttime. Sorrow seemed to envelop him. I knew he needed me the most then. I would just lie by his side on the wooden bench atop the deck with my head resting on his leg. I would have preferred to lie in his lap, but I weighed fifty pounds, so I am not actually great lap dog material like rodent dog.

One night, he told me that the house beside us was where his childhood friend, Nicky Pipkin, grew up and how they probably played ball on the land our house was built on.

He reminisced quite often. Sometimes it was about good things like Nicky. He told me that Nicky was the most intelligent person in their grade at nearby Bradley Creek Elementary School. Not the school where it is located today but the old one that burned down years ago. He told me that he bet Nicky was a doctor or something important. I don't think that he meant an animal doctor—pretty sure that he meant some kind of people doctor.

He would smile as he rubbed my thick black hair. I guess I should have informed you earlier that I am a mixed breed dog. I have a lot of black lab in me, but I also have long, thick hair that rules out my being purebred. My master thought I might be part Golden Retriever. He informed me once that he didn't care what parts made up my DNA—because I was all heart.

"I bet Nicky is still the same humble boy that I grew up with," he would say with a wistful smile. "I wonder where he is. We lost touch when we were bused to ninth-grade centers in 1971. The dividing line was Oleander Drive, and though we only lived a half-mile apart, I don't think I have seen Nicky since the last day of school at Roland-Grise Junior High when we were anxious to leave the eighth grade behind and be kings of the school the following academic year. But the school board made a pressurized decision one month before school was to begin, and we were bused to what was previously a predominately black school to achieve racial integration.

"We resented it at the time, but it was the right thing, Pete. At the time, I was too young and prone to believe the stereotypes placed unfairly on people to understand.

"Truthfully, we would have lost contact anyway. Nicky kept studying and playing sports, and I started hanging out at the pool room doing all sorts of things that I should not have done. Bad things that Nicky was wise enough to avoid."

I don't know what stereotypes mean or even integration, for that matter. I realize now that people were different colors, and I think maybe it has something to do with that, though I can tell you my master never cared about color. One of his favorite people in the world is Richard. He and Richard coached boys together in a city basketball league. Richard came to our home often. He was a nice man, and my master loved him.

I recalled something that took place with Cody when he was still a little guy. I guess come to think of it, he was always a little guy when I was with them. My master had two friends named Richard. The other man was Richard Busby. My master informed Cody that Richard was coming over that night. Cody inquired as to whether it was black Richard or white Richard.

My master shook his head and replied, "I don't see it that way. I just see my two friends."

Cody was insistent and queried him once again. He received the same answer. I believe that my master saw this as to what is sometimes referred to as a teachable moment.

Cody tried once again and shaped his question in another manner. "Is it the Richard that coaches with you?"

My master answered, "Yes."

Cody thought for a while, narrowed his eyes, and stated in a low voice, "Well, he is black, Dad." My master turned away from his precious son, but I saw him chuckling slightly as he tried to keep control over the moment of instruction. He shared the story with his coaching friend later that night, and they both derived a good chortle out of the story.

I so hated leaving my master. He was alone a lot, and he had all these dreams that never panned out. He would talk to me about it in the wee hours of the morning when the silence of the night's despair kept him from being able to find respite. Now, I always loved sleeping. I was known to give an exasperated sigh if there was too much noise in the house when I was bedding down for the night, but I put my love of sleep aside for those nights when he really needed me. He would share with me the guilt that he felt from his failures and broken dreams. It was dreadful those many nights that Cody was with his mom. He missed that little boy so much that I am not sure there are words that would ever convey that and lend it justice. I only wish that I could have helped remove his anguish, but all I could do was comfort him the best that I knew how.

There was a girl that he dated for a while after he was freshly divorced. I don't recall her name. I do remember that she was a real dog lover. She had two of her own, and I think they were both some kind of Terrier.

The first time she came into our house—I rose from the corner where I was sleeping to greet my master and inspect her. She saw something in my eyes and remarked with absolute conviction, "My gosh, that dog simply adores you. Look at the way she looks at you." I know what that word adore means now, and she picked the perfect word. I did adore my master. Even when he took some of his anger out towards me. There was nothing that man could have done to tarnish my love for him.

A flock of birds greeted me with song as they landed nearby. I can't identify all of them, but I am certain that I see Blue Jays, Cardinals, Sparrows, Carolina Wrens, and a bird with black, white, and red colors. I believe that to be a Rose-breasted Grosbeak. I know you are impressed with my knowledge of birds, but I have been here for quite some time, and I have become educated on many things.

Everything is pretty much perfect in this place—well, with the obvious exception of my master not being here. It is better than people can even imagine. I see the glow, the joy as they walked through the gate in disbelief. People say that they believe, but I am not certain that many believe to the extent of a place so magnificent as this. Heaven may be without ugliness or difficulty, but that does not mean all of us—both human and pet who made it are instantly flawless. We have to learn things as well, and I think that is the way it should be.

One of the shepherds—no, not a German Shepherd but an authentic shepherd, was walking up the hill toward me. His name is Amos, and he strolled at a nice leisurely pace. He had a staff in one hand and a rod in the other, which I find humorous because there has not been a lost sheep or an attack on any animal—at least as far back as since I arrived.

He was in front of me now. He wore a deep blue and white robe, right out of the Old Testament, which was only proper as that was his time on earth. I have often annoyed him with questions, and he would give one stern shake of his head to the left, and I learned not to inquire on the subject again. It wasn't like he was going to answer me anyway.

"Petra, you are needed at the entrance gate. Please walk with me," he said as he began walking toward the village.

"Is it—"

He turned back to me, and he gave a half a shake of his head to the left and said nothing. I guess I only received half of a dismissive headshake since I ceased mid-way with my question. If you were paying attention—you recall my telling you that while we may live in an impeccable paradise—we still are learning. We always will be, and that is good. No one likes a know it all—regardless of where they reside.

Before we venture deeper into this story—I guess that I should explain something to you. I don't audibly talk but somehow when I want to communicate, I am heard clearly. That does not mean all my thoughts are converted to speaking words. It took me some time to understand that this was happening. Please don't ask me to explain it all. Only God can, and from what I have been told, the last time he was asked by one of the animals—he just erupted in warm laughter. He laughs a lot. I am not sure that fits in with the perception people have of him.

We walked through the East Village. Amos stopped and pointed to the entrance gate. "There is a little fella that is going to be coming down the hill in just a few moments. He is going to be uncertain about what is transpiring. I want you to greet him and help him along the way.

16

Remember his memories of what has transpired are going to be raw. Be very gentle with him."

"Is he a person or a pet?"

"Pet."

Okay, that was a little disappointing, but I kept that to myself. He did say little fella, and my master was over six feet tall and lifted weights in the cramped garage five days a week when I was with him. Little he was not. "How will I know him?" Chalk one up for me because that is two outstanding inquiries because he did not do the head shake to either question. He almost smiled.

"His name is Sydny."

"How will I know?" I thought that to be a very legitimate question, but believe it or not, I got the left only head shake.

"Faith, Petra. We have eternity. You don't have to try and figure everything out."

Amos occasionally irritated the poop out of me even though we don't do that here. He knows dang well that I am disappointed that I am not coming to greet my master. Wouldn't you be? I have never previously been instructed to go to the entrance gate. He gets my hopes up like this and for what?

My words may not be audible right now, but that does not mean that Amos does not comprehend my feelings on the matter. He crouched on one knee and rubbed my head. "Petra, I know this is not what you hoped it to be but take care of this little guy, and perhaps he might just provide answers to some of your questions."

I think I did a brief headshake to the left.

"Petra, you do realize where I received this particular directive, don't you?"

Did I just do another miniature head shake to the left? Gosh, I don't want to become irritating like Amos.

People have positions here, including Amos, but I think this particular order came straight from the top. Now, I am beyond curious. Still, I must take care of my task first. I don't want this Sydny to have a welcoming partner like I did. I am still not sure how Amanda even made it. She is still a roaming, crazed beagle even in Heaven. More about her later.

"You are one of the best we have here, Petra. I have every confidence that you will do a stellar job," Amos said.

Okay, my vocabulary is still not flawless, and I am not sure about this word stellar. Still, from his expression, I am going to assume that it is a good thing.

Amos shared information that I would need to know to aid Sydny in adjusting to his new home. He patted me once on top of my head and walked away.

I begin making my way up the hill.

2 ~ Sydny

Carolina Beach is overrun with feral cats and some of our neighbors have made it their life calling to feed them. I made it my life calling that when they ventured into our yard to chase them back from whence they came.

My human dad—I possess no knowledge of who my dog parents were. It is obvious to look at me that Chihuahua dominates my bloodline, but I am bigger than a Chihuahua, mostly black, and one of my endearing physical qualities, according to my dad, Cole Banks, is that I have ears like a German Shepherd.

I know he exaggerates somewhat, okay, maybe even a lot on occasion, but I have viewed myself in the mirror, and the truth is that I do have big ears. Still, he likes them, and though I never had a dad until late in my life—it is vital to me what he thinks. For the first nine years of my life—after a very rough beginning—I lived with my mom, Ava.

Perhaps later, I will share what I remember from those early days, but for now, you are probably wondering what the stray cats have to do with this story. It seems like a few weeks ago, but with all that has occurred, I have lost the concept of time—not that I ever actually comprehended it. Currently, I can recall a lot of events clearly. I wish it were not so. I am a dog—so most of our happiness is built around simplistic desires. Humans seem so stressed that I can't understand why they don't learn from us. As I am departing the life I knew and loved, there are many things I will miss. My mom and rescuer the most, but my dad is not far behind.

I am already missing observing him with keen eyes as he scrambled eggs with a little bit of pepper jack cheese mixed in. He always shared with me. Mom got a little upset with him at times because she was worried about my weight. But deep down, I am confident that it pleased her that we had both fallen in love with each other.

It was not easy. I never knew much love except from mom and her parents. Mom rescued me from a ghastly future—actually it held no potential as I was about to be put down. That is a nice term for euthanasia. I guess it was my fault. I bit people. It was my defense mechanism. The word used frequently about me was unadoptable.

I was wary of people. I did not like strangers touching me regardless of how cute I may be, and trust me, big ears or not, I am simply adorable. Keep your doggone hands to yourself was my motto. It is not like I did not give them fair warning. My dad figured it out right away. I did not stare the potential threat down. If I was looking directly at someone—all was well, but if I turned my head to the side, and my upper left lip curled up slightly, followed by an almost soundless snarl, they were in trouble. I don't know what triggered my response. It was not as if they were mean to me. But once my top left lip arched slightly—they had about three seconds to get their paws off of me. Paws— isn't that funny? I realize that humans don't have paws. That is sad. They don't know what they are missing. I can't imagine being able to scratch a terrible itch with their inept equipment.

Dad loves dogs, and in particular, he prefers Labrador Retrievers. I heard him often speak of Pete. There is a beautiful portrait of her in his office. I have no understanding of how a beautiful, long-haired female mixed lab came to be known as Pete.

Strangely, when they began dating—he had no dogs at his house. Pete had been gone for a long time. I heard him say to mom once. "It hurt too bad to dig that hole and say goodbye. I don't want to feel that pain ever again."

Don't get me wrong. He was always kind to me. He loves my mom so much that he would do just about anything in his power to make her happy. He realized right from the beginning that it was a package deal.

I had to break him in slowly. He was way too uptight when he was solely responsible for watching over me. He worried so much, that at times, his care of me proved a bit stifling. Dad seemed that way about everything. He takes responsibility and loyalty very seriously. Often, I wanted to tell him to chill. After all, I was a tough dog, who grew up on the streets.

Let me tell you about the night I charged the big dog next door. I could hear Dad calling frantically for me and then for my mom when he could not convince me to return. He was afraid I would get hurt by the dog that was four times my size or run out in the street and possibly be struck by a car. But doggonit that oversized collie had wandered into our yard. What else was I supposed to do?

The owner of the collie called out over the bushes. "Cole, Sydney is right here. He chased my dog back in the yard and now he is peeing on my trees."

I was peeing on the third tree while eyeing that dog and making darn sure he knew what was what. Dad looked over the hedge and spoke sternly, "Sydney, you come here right now." He apologized to the neighbor, who did not appear upset in the least. "Don't worry about it," the man replied with a wave of his hand as he resumed drinking his can of beer without an apparent care in the world.

I finished peeing, though at this point it was more for show than bodily function. By now, Mom was outside as well and calling urgently for me. I offered one last stern look to that collie and sauntered back to my yard with my head held high. That terrified collie never ventured into our yard again.

Dad and Mom said all those things that parents say. Don't do that again. How badly I had frightened them. You know the drill.

Dad scooped me up and held me close. I could feel his heart thumping, and I knew that he was truly afraid that something bad could have happened to me.

Okay, I promise you that I will not deviate any longer from telling you about the cats. Dad taught me to chase the cats off our property. I was more than happy to do this as I never lived where we had any land before. Plus, you should have seen how much my dad glowed when I did my job suitably. I grew to love making that man happy. Mom acted like she disapproved, but I observed her slight smile. Most of all, she loved that this man that made her beam, as I had never witnessed prior, was becoming more attached to me with each passing day. It was hard for either of us to do much wrong in her eyes.

This particular late summer morning—we walked out the front door so that I could do my business. Dad spotted a tabby cat that must have weighed twenty pounds. That made it two of me, except when Dad fed me too much from the table and my weight crept up to eleven pounds. Mom would get on him, and he would say that it was only one pound. She said something about ten percent, but one thing dad and I have in common is that we don't like math very much. Shoot, I don't even know what a percent is.

"Cat, Syd." I heard him say in his command voice, and I was off and running. I was sprinting harder and faster than I ever had in my life. I was so youthful and happy.

Oh, how I wish you could have seen how proud he looked. The cat was long gone from our yard. I was not supposed to continue the chase past our property. I stopped and turned around and saw him smiling and waving for me to return. But as often occurs when one sprints, it loosened my bowels, and I had to—well, you know—no need to get too graphic here. I finished, and he walked toward me with a tan grocery bag in his hand. The man even cleans up after me. I think it is readily apparent who derives the most from this affiliation.

I saw this pit or a nut on the ground. Now, I did not need to eat it. I had already been fed my dog food, and I had noticed Dad take the eggs out—crack them open into a bowl and add some water and spices. We were going to have eggs. Still, once you have been a starving dog—it never entirely leaves you. I ate that thing as he was shouting at me to leave it. It did not taste good, and I barely got it down. This ominous feeling came over me, and somehow, I knew that I had committed a horrendous misstep.

The next few weeks passed by and all was well. It has proven to be a good life since Mom rescued me. I never worried about being hungry again. I was grateful for the food and water but in our first year together, I did not care about this love she kept insisting on doling out on me. She would insist on kissing my face. Even when I snarled at her, she talked firmly but soothingly to me.

She could have chosen to return me to the place in Southern Pines, North Carolina, that she rescued me from, but she never considered it. She refused to give up on me. I am so thankful for that now. Our lives were intertwined for nine years. It was just us and sometimes a roommate. Some of them were okay, and some were just downright flakey. I was not particularly fond of any of them.

During that time that it was just us. She was lonely a lot, and she prayed all the time about her Boaz and where he was at? I had no clue who this Boaz was. We grew closer as the years rolled by, and I realized I could trust this wonderful, kind-hearted woman with all of my heart. I still was not very pleasant with other people. No danger of me winning a Miss Congeniality contest, and for goodness sakes, I am a boy dog, so the whole Miss thing would not even begin to work. There were several people that I was forced to give the sideway snarl to. I may have even nipped at a few hands along the way. Please don't think badly of me.

The only part I did not like during that period in our lives was when she would leave me to go to work. I hated being alone in that apartment. She never could afford a house. Still, she came home every day at lunch to walk me and allow me to do my business, but mostly she came home to spend time with me. There were times it felt as if I was her entire world. Still, at night while I was tucked safely in the bed with her, I would hear her sniffling, and I knew that she was crying. At times it was more than my little heart could bear.

I would nestle closer to her and put my face right near hers. That was my ultimate sign of confidence.

The holidays seemed to be especially difficult for her, particularly Christmas. We often ventured outside at night during that time. I thought it was to look at the Christmas decorations, but in retrospect, I think that she just thought it a better avenue to converse with God.

She would often dress me in a sweater for these outings if the weather was the least bit nippy. I am predominately Chihuahua, and I shiver when it is seventy-two degrees. I was the best dressed dog in the neighborhood. Oh, I probably could have won a couple of tacky Christmas sweater contests, but the main thing I am trying to convey to you is that she always made sure I was warm. She even tucked me inside her coat to add protection on really cold evenings.

We would sit on a bench or chair—whatever was available, and she would hold me tight. She would speak to God and ask him if she was to remain alone forever. She had so much love she wanted to give to the right man this time. Mom was married once before, and it ended shortly before she rescued me. Maybe that was one of the reasons she decided she wanted me. She already had another dog, Savanna—a pure-bred brindle Chihuahua. I will tell you about her a little later in the story.

What I can ascertain is this. She wed at a young age and spent much of her marriage neglected and feeling unloved. I knew what not being cared for felt like—especially now that I know how great it is to have someone love you. What kind of dopey man would not love my mom? That is a rhetorical question if you did not know that already. Still, I think I would be remiss not to answer the question. A complete idiot—that is who. Mom is so beautiful, and she has these gorgeous big hazel eyes. They are so full of tenderness, kindness, compassion, and when she looked at me and said that I was the best seventy-five dollars that she ever spent—my little heart melted.

Oh, and did I mention how wonderfully she sings? I really enjoyed the weeks when she was scheduled to sing in church. She would practice at home, and I loved being her only audience.

I observed her help others when she barely had enough to feed herself. During one period she ate these Ramen noodles mixed in with a few vegetables for one solid month because she had no money. I felt so sorry for her. I know you might not believe this, but I would have shared my food with her that cost way more than those noodles, but she never skimped on my dog food and bought something less expensive. Not one time. There were times that if I could have talked that I would have told her to buy the cheaper food. The vet told her this was what I needed to eat and so that was that. Mom would do without so that I could eat properly.

Being as self-absorbed as I am there were times that I resented that I did not seem to be enough for her life. However, I learned that even a faithful dog does not fill every desire that a woman holds in her heart.

I hated to ever see her unhappy, and I hoped that God would indeed send my mom a Boaz. Boaz—what a peculiar name. I worried though, what would happen to a somewhat rude dog such as me if God did send this bizarrely named man into our lives?

Remember how I told you about that eerie feeling that I had when I ate that pit? I felt pretty good most of the time during the next few weeks, though sometimes when Dad picked me up, I would yelp. He was befuddled as he always gathered me so gently. Maybe God should have allowed dogs to speak. I could have said, "Hey, Dad— remember that day I ate that thing on the ground? It is stuck, and I can feel it at times, especially when you touch that spot. I don't mean to growl at you. I'm sorry I even nipped like I was going to bite you. I would not do that."

I may be brave enough to charge dogs ten times my size. No, I am not talking about that dang collie. There was a boxer dog strolling through the neighborhood one day when Mom was tending to the flowers in our front yard. That boxer about peed himself after I charged at him for daring to venture near Mom, however, I did not feel so courageous about that pit. It was stuck and try as I might, I could not strain enough to allow it to pass. Mom and Dad often wondered why I insisted on trying to poop even after I had already done my daily allotment. I even tried to make myself gag and throw it up, but that proved futile as well.

There was one other thing bothering me. My nose was running, and I heard Mom mention a heart murmur. Savanna suffered from it for years until she had to be put down because of it. I like the idea that despite the heart murmur she lived till the ripe old age of seventeen. I really want six more years, but in my heart, I knew my time was limited. Mom is going to be so upset. She cried a lot when Savanna died, and I know that in time she loved me even more. I don't mean that statement to boast. There are some things a dog just knows.

I was privy to a lot of conversations when my mom and dad met. I did not understand as much of it as I seem to at the present time. One thing I could clearly understand is that they enjoyed being together, and that they dearly loved each other.

Dad was older than Mom by seventeen years. I don't know how that equates to dog years but in human years it must be a lot. What I can suffice is that it never bothered Mom, but it sure did trouble Dad. He worried about getting old and leaving her behind. When he talked like that, it just broke Mom's heart. Mom loves so deeply but you know what? Dad does as well. He learned in time not to say such things, and when he felt that way around her, I think he just kept it to himself, or if it was just the two of us, he shared his concerns with me. I never told a soul.

Another unfortunate part with this pit and heart murmur talk is that Dad and I have not even had two full years together. We have shared a lot of time together, especially the past fourteen months after he quit his part-time job at the Fort Fisher Aquarium. I have let down all my defenses around this man, and he has allowed me fully into his heart as well.

I am such a part of his day now that Mom acts a bit jealous of how I love being near him even when she comes home from work. My favorite is when he lays on the couch, and I nestled in on his left hip. My preferred time is nap time, and that is where I love to be, especially when it is cold. And when it is hot—I lie down real close to his face on the other side of the L shaped sectional couch when we enjoy afternoon nap time. He often looked over and kissed me right on the side of my face. I don't even think about biting him.

He is that tender with me, but he is also my protector. I go to Mom when I am sick, but when I am afraid, like now, I want to be near him. One confession from this small, feisty dog—I have always been deathly afraid of thunderstorms. I can sense them ten minutes before that first clap of thunder.

My bed was in the living room during the first month they were married. They seemed to want to be alone a lot for reasons that I don't understand. I did not like that one bit. It was too far away and besides that, I was accustomed to sleeping in the bed. Don't get me wrong. I loved my bed. It looked like a miniature version of some beds for humans that I have seen. As the morning light first peeped in, I would lie outside the closed bedroom door and wait. Dad was an early riser. I wanted him to think that I had suffered just outside that door all night on the hardwood floors with no cushion.

He broke as I knew that he would. My bed was placed on Mom's side of the bed, right under the window. I was safe. Well, until those dang thunderstorms started erupting. Booms followed by lightning that lit up the entire room like it was the middle of the day.

When I sensed a storm approaching, I would walk past Mom around to his side of the bed. Mom could sleep through a train running through the backyard. I know we don't have tracks in the backyard or anywhere on the island, for that matter, but I am telling a story, so grant me a little leeway, please.

The bed was high, so I would paw frantically as far up as I could reach. He always heard me right away. He never fussed when I woke him. He would pick me up and put me between Mom and him under the covers. I would try to burrow under the covers as far as I could get, but he did not like that because he was concerned that he might roll over on me. He taught me how to sleep like they did, and often I would prop my head on one side of his pillow, and he would be on the other.

He would hold me firmly during the storm and whisper repeatedly, "Syd, I got you. I am not going to let anything harm you." My trembling didn't depart immediately, but he sure did help calm me.

It was amazing how much wiser I am becoming since I succumbed to that stupid pit. Oh, I don't understand everything, but in reflection, many things add up now that did not before as I reflect on my last good time on earth.

He has told me many times of late that I am going to the beach with them in October. That is the time of year that dogs are allowed on the beach all day. He wants the temps to cool down some for me so I won't get too hot. It all sounds great.

I was ten years old before I saw the beach, and I could understand why my dad loved it so much. It was beautiful, and that sand under my feet felt so good. Still, Dad best understand doggone well that I am not venturing into the ocean. That thing is huge— and the noise it makes. No sir. Count me out. I will watch Dad swim from the beach.

I suppose that I have delayed long enough. It is time to tell you about that last weekend I spent with Mom and Dad. You might want to get a tissue out.

It was Friday morning, and Mom was in Wilmington helping someone with an organization project. It was just Dad and me. We sat on the couch together, and he rose to take care of his business. Dad walked to the bathroom. It was just a number one, so don't feel the need to cover your ears. I followed right behind him.

Ever since I ate that pit, I have been afraid to let him out of my sight. He has noticed my behavior, and once again this morning, he saw me in the doorway watching. "Syd, what is the matter, boy?" I wanted to tell him that I knew my time was short, and I just felt more secure to be where I could see him—to hear the gentle nature of his voice.

He walked toward me and asked if I wanted to go outside. I hopped the playful way I often did in answer to his question. We walked outside, and a black cat was on our front porch. I took off after it in full pursuit. I ran it right into the neighbor's yard. Not the one with the collie—but the other side. I ran into their front yard, and that cat had rounded the corner and was hiding under the shed in the backyard. My task was complete. But at the end of my sprint, I felt that pit dislodge. I just knew it could not be good. It wasn't.

We were back inside of our home when I left Dad and walked into the guest room to get sick. Dad sensed something was wrong, and he went looking for me. I could hear him calling my name. I was ashamed that I had messed up the floor so badly. It looked like a lake where I got sick.

Dad found me. "What's the matter, boy?" He knew something was amiss because I never left one room to go to another when I was with him. He saw what I had done, and I thought that he might be mad at me. I could not have been more wrong. "Oh, Syd," he said wearily as he dropped his head. He loved on me and told me that it was okay, and then he went to get a roll of paper towels, and he cleaned up the mess I had done.

We walked into the living room, and he sat in his recliner and coaxed me to come to him and as he picked me up—I yelped in pain. He cradled me and sat in the recliner with me. I looked in his eyes, and this big tough man had tears streaming down his face to such a degree it reminded me of a waterfall that I saw right before Mom and Dad began dating. She had taken me to the mountains to visit her Uncle Garfield. We saw a waterfall that had a stream of water cascading down the stones about one foot wide. His tears broke my heart.

He called Mom, and they talked for several minutes. I think that she was trying to reassure him that I had been sick before and that a bit of rice and broth once the vomiting passed would help my stomach.

Dad said he was going to call the Animal Hospital. They told him that it sounded like I had just caught a bug but that if my stomach did not settle to bring me in. I know Dad said all the right things about how they were right, and I was just a little sick, but the look in his eyes told me that he knew better. I also knew that in time he was going to blame himself for not taking me immediately to see the vet. I know this as well as I know that Mom would feel guilty for not coming home right away.

I did not understand his next course of action. He gently got up and left me on the recliner. He came back with a tiny bottle of oil. He gingerly sat back down as I moved to the side. He allowed me to get back into his lap on my own so I could do it with the least amount of pain. I was grateful for that because regardless of how tenderly he picked me up, it hurt like the dickens.

He prayed for me—and at one point, he dabbed his finger with this oil, and he marked out the cross on my head. He prayed for a long time. I think he prayed all day. That day I found out that as much as he loved me, there was a depth to his love that I never fully comprehended. Mom loved me so much longer, but I think that Dad loved me every bit as much in the end.

I didn't get sick again for a while. He called the Animal Hospital again and they suggested he try feeding me the rice and broth. I watched as he prepared a dish that I knew I could not keep down. But you know what? By the time the food was ready, even I had a sliver of hope when I discovered that I was hungry. I ate a small bowl. Mom and the lady at the Animal Hospital had instructed Dad just to give me a little bit. They told dad if I went an hour and a half without getting sick that I was probably out of the woods, and this bug had passed. That was ridiculous. Even I wouldn't eat a bug.

Dad watched that clock so anxiously. He tried to busy himself doing other things, but he didn't fool me one little bit. The clock passed an hour, and a sliver of light appeared in his eyes. At one hour and forty minutes, I was still holding the rice down. He called Mom in his excitement and even more his relief.

Dad went into his office for a few minutes. I left my bed in the living room to drink a little water. That is when I got sick again—right by the front door. Dad returned a few minutes later—by now, I was back in my bed. He knelt and loved on me and spoke so encouragingly. I saw the hope in his eyes. Why did I have to eat that pit?

He walked into the kitchen for something, and that is when he noticed the rice and broth on the floor. He dropped his head and you could literally see the hope draining out of him. He retrieved his phone off the counter.

"Ava, you better come home now," he said softly. "We are taking him to the vet."

Mom rushed home and they took me to the Animal Hospital. They examined me and hooked this tube to my body to provide fluids that I was lacking. They scheduled a follow up appointment for early the next morning.

That night Dad did a peculiar thing. He moved my bed over to his side of the bedroom. I could not sleep much as that pit hurt so severely, and I don't think Mom and Dad did either, especially Dad. Several times he looked at me during the night, and often he got up to kneel and talk with me. He would rub me so gently. How a man so big could be so tender is something I don't understand, but that is my dad.

I threw up in my bed during the night. By now, it looked almost like water as there was nothing of substance remaining in me. Dad and I walked outside at the first full light of the day. He shuffled beside me as I moved so slowly. I cocked my leg out of habit, but I am not sure anything came out. We went back inside the house, and Mom was drinking coffee. She gave a mug of it to Dad. There was no breakfast being cooked. A suffocating silence reigned throughout our home.

Dad sat in his recliner by the window and retrieved his Bible off the table beside it. I watched him try to concentrate and read, but I knew his mind was wandering. I also knew that this was the last morning that I would spend in this house with the people I held so tightly in my heart. I walked over to him. I looked up and did a slow circle.

Mom was watching. "He wants to be up there with you." It was my morning ritual to sit with him as he read his Bible.

"It will hurt him if I pick him up."

"It is what he wants."

She walked over to me without another word and gingerly picked me up and placed me on his lap. It was worth all the pain.

They took me to the Animal Hospital soon after devotion. They used this machine that could see inside my body, and I heard them say a pit was lodged in my small intestine. I wish I could have talked. I would have told them myself what it was and saved my parents a lot of money. The following words were surgery.

Mom and Dad picked me up late that afternoon. The pit was gone and the vet seemed hopeful. They were encouraged to have me spend the night in an overnight emergency clinic where they could better monitor me. During the ride, I laid in Mom's lap and looked up at Dad in my drug-induced state as he drove quietly into the fading sunlight. Boy, was I going to miss him and our rides together. I waited a long time for a dad and did not even care to have one but boy, when I got one—he was the best. I would take nothing for our time together. I just hated to see the injury in his eyes. I wanted to place my paw on his arm one last time like I often did. Dad looked at me several times on the ride, but he remained silent.

They took me inside. Mom filled out paperwork and someone gave dad yet another bill and then they left me with the promise that they were returning in the morning. I wanted so badly to go home with them. It would have been easier for all of us. They would realize that in time, and they would feel tremendous remorse for leaving me there.

There were a lot of other animals in individual cages. They give me a shot of something, and I went to sleep peacefully—dreaming about Dad and Mom taking me to the beach. It was October, and the ocean was calm, and the sky was royal blue. It was warm but not hot like in the summer, and believe it or not—I went into the ocean with Dad. The water felt good. He held me tight, and I was unafraid. My protector always. Mom stood on the beach—watching us and laughing.

We looked out in the ocean, and thirty yards in front of us, seven dolphins were circling and playing. I did not know what to make of that, but I knew they would not hurt us.

And then I felt myself above the cage and I was drifting upwards…

31

3 ~ David Hill

I sat in the most comfortable worn rocking chair on the balcony of our cottage while reading the Bible. It may be Heaven but the word never perishes—never is it not relevant, even in this majestic place. I am reading from the book of Micah. It contains one of my favorite verses. *Micah 6:8 He has showed you, O man, what is good; and what does the LORD require of you, but to do justly, and to love mercy, and to walk humbly with your God?*

Lifting my head, I gazed out at the scenery. As much as I loved to sit in my earthly home and look out over Banks Channel at Wrightsville Beach it does not hold a candle to this landscape. The waterway is calm, peaceful, inviting, and full of activity. Sailboats pushed by a persistently favorable breeze, while others enjoy paddling canoes. People are everywhere but as strange as it may sound no one gets in anyone's way. It is crowded and yet there is room for everyone. I guess back on earth that would be a strange quote. It certainly helps that no one is in a rush to arrive at their next destination. They are already here.

Beyond the open waters, there are secluded marsh areas with multiple creeks winding through the landscape. Men and women seated in colorful kayaks paddled through the creeks, enjoying the scenery and the plethora of beautiful birds that call these marshlands home. And yet there always seems to be a creek just for you if one decides to soak in solitude. I am so deeply engrossed in my observations that it took me a moment to realize that someone is sitting in the chair beside me.

I turned and it is Jesus. You can't help but smile when your Lord is sitting casually next to you like a comfortable friend. He motioned toward the Bible in my lap. "You did well to live Micah 6:8. It is a shame that more people, especially ministers chose not to. Many times, I have blessed a ministry only to have the leader's egos grow to the point where it became more about them than it did the Gospel."

"Pride goes before destruction, and a haughty spirit before a fall," I offered, before pondering if it is somewhat silly to quote scripture to the one who inspired such writings.

The Lord did not respond as he peered out at the waters. Talk about a peace that passes all understanding. I experienced that at times before I arrived here, but it was always interrupted and never as potent as it is at this very moment. I am after all sitting beside my Savior.

"I tell you little of what goes on back there."

"Is there something that you need to tell me about now, Lord? Is it one of my sons?"

"Not by blood," he said with a smile that reminded me of the most vivid rainbows that you could imagine.

I waited for him to continue. Two men raced each other in sailboats and we could hear their laughter. There are no losers in this place. You have won the ultimate prize just by making it here.

"Cole Banks. His favorite scripture is Micah 6:8. He lives it far better than he thinks he does."

"That son," I answered. "We had so little time together, but it always meant so much to both of us."

"Rarely a day passes that he does not reflect about you."

"Why did he gravitate towards me to such a degree?"

"Your encouragement. Your lack of judgement."

I nodded gently.

"He is humble but yet he does not come under authority all that well."

I knew this to be true. I deliberated for a few moments. "Is that a downfall for him?"

"Sometimes—but it also may well be one of his greatest assets."

"I always appreciated that what you saw with Cole is what you got. I received enough of the other side of that as a minister."

"Cole has had two mentors in his life. The first was his baseball coach, Ed Wilson, who I orchestrated a way for him to be the vessel that would rescue Cole from a life of destruction."

There was silence for several moments as we both rested our eyes on the water.

"You said two mentors, Lord?"

"The other is you."

I nodded my head gently with great appreciation. "He always was so hard on himself. I think that is why he had no time for those that judged him."

"He is still his worst critic, but he has come so far, and as I told you long ago, he bows to me now. It took a long time but one day shortly after events I arranged for him to attend Passion in Atlanta—he was driving down the road and he said, "Take the wheel, Lord. We have him now forever, David. He will never stray again.""

"But he is in trouble, Lord?"

"He and Ava are hurting right now. I will show you why. Walk with me."

We rose and soon we were at the edge of the water. "Let's walk across."

I laughed joyously.

"Take my hand," he gently offered.

I was like a small child as I walked across the water with him. I could not stop giggling and the Lord said, "Oh, what a joy you are."

Our feet found purchase on the shore and then we walked through the village and arrived at a balcony. Rarely is this permitted. I recalled how honored I was that day that I was allowed to sit and watch Cole and Ava's wedding. Another warm reflection visited from my time before. I am not sure how all that works. We don't recall everything because let's face it there were a lot of less pleasant times that we all endured.

I chuckled and asked, "You just brought that memory to mind for me, didn't you?"

He laughed heartily. "Yes. When you were older Cole bought his house at Carolina Beach, and he knew that you could not come to him."

"He called me and asked if I could do him a favor. I could not think of anything I could do for him in my weakened condition, and he reassured me when I voiced that. He said, 'Oh, you can do this one. He wanted me to pray over his new house."

"He loved you way more than you ever realized, David. He still does. Let's sit."

My Lord opened the top of the sky and I gazed down. I expected to see Cole but I did not. A mixed-breed Chihuahua dog was sleeping in a cage in a hospital.

"They check him hourly. It is three a.m. and the lady that is checking him will return soon and he will be gone.

"Is he coming here?"

"Would I have you here if it were not so?"

I shook my head in dismay at my foolish question. We watched quietly as the lady returned just as my Lord said.

She checked him and discovered that he was not breathing. Frantically, she called for the doctor. He came and checked the little dog's vitals and softly shook his head.

The lady asked hurriedly, "Do we resuscitate?"

"It will do no good. Sydny is gone. Call his parents."

And just like that, the hole in the sky closed and the viewing was over. Next, the Lord filled me in on all I would need to know to carry out the task he requested. As always, I was honored and humbled to do so.

4 ~ Cole Banks

I was not optimistic about Sydny's chances. My wonderful wife, Ava, kept praying and believing. I will tell you right now that she has more faith than I do. Don't get me wrong. Mine is not subpar. My beginning with God was walking down a dark road one night as a very young troubled man. I felt this whoosh that went through me from the top of my head to the bottom of my feet and then I heard, *"Come and admit you're wrong. Come and sing my beautiful song."* Such a statement had never been spoken by or to me or ever crossed my mind.

Even after that glorious Damascus Road born again experience and subsequently falling away from God for decades in a bitter rage, in which, I blamed him for much of my troubles—I never was able to escape that night. I returned to him a few years ago and my anger has dissipated and been replaced by a far more tranquil way of life.

We would always regret leaving Sydny alone in that overnight clinic. We could have taken care of him as well as they did but we were encouraged to leave him—after all we had already invested so much money for the surgery is what we were told. We understood with the passage of time that Sydny was never going to survive the surgery.

They did not check his heart to see if it was strong enough to survive surgery. I know this because there would have been another bill for that. They just threw that $1200 figure out for surgery knowing we would most likely go forward with it.

That night as Sydny laid at that emergency clinic, I moved his bed into the spare bedroom. Ava had a premonition right then that I knew he was not coming back to us alive. Maybe that is true but I knew each time I woke I could not look at that empty bed. I took some melatonin to help me get some sleep, and I was so exhausted that it actually worked.

My phone rested on the bed stand and at three-thirty in the still

37

darkness of the morning it began to ring. "No, no, no. No, God. No," I declared desperately.

Ava was awake by now and as I took the phone and said, "Yes." She was already asking questions.

The only real words that I can recall from this brief conversation was that Sydny stopped breathing. She asked me about cremation and I answered no—we would come to gather our furry child.

The phone call ended–my wife so distraught. Her voice so filled in anguish. "I don't understand," she kept repeating. We sobbed for several minutes and when we were able to catch our breath—I will not forget what she said next.

"You spent all that money, and he did not make it. Almost two thousand dollars and for what? I am so sorry."

When we were giving the figures for the surgery—I never balked for one second. Ava told me it was my decision and she would understand. All I could picture was how that day—was it just two days ago now? Sydny chasing that cat. So full of energy and in a few short hours—he was gone.

I don't know why I answered my wife the way I did. But I looked at her and said softly but firmly, "Never mention the money again. I have no regrets. It would have been worth every penny to have him back with us. I would do it all over again. Never feel bad about it. That little guy was about way more than money."

Before dawn arrived, she said, "Let's go get our boy."

I am supposed to be this big tough man, but I will share this with you, and I hope that you will not think less of me. We drove into the parking lot of the emergency clinic. I put my truck in park and left the motor idling. I looked straight ahead—cloaked in my shame—I could not face my wife at that moment.

"I hope that you can understand this, but I can't go inside. I just can't."

I was afraid that she would try to persuade me or tell me how much she needed me to go with her. There were no words she could have spoken that would have moved me from gripping that steering wheel and staring blankly into the darkness.

My beautiful wife knows me well enough to understand that there was no room for debate in my words. She touched my arm and said softly, "I understand." I heard the door close as I sat in the gloom of that early morning.

There were faint rays of light when we returned home with Sydny in a box. I buried him in our courtyard. Ava stood several feet away, unable to participate. I requested that she toss the first shovel of dirt on top of him. I don't know why I did this, but I thought it important at the time. She did that and then she walked away and said, "I can't do this part. I just can't." I nodded my head in understanding and granted her the same grace that she had permitted me several minutes earlier.

I have dug three holes for dogs in my life. Amanda, my crazy beagle—Pete, the dog above all dogs, and now the little Chihuahua mix, who was as large a dog as I have ever witnessed. Each time a piece of me went down in the hole that I would never regain.

Over the next several weeks we were asked repeatedly when we were getting another dog. I didn't want another dog. I wanted Sydny back.

The intense grief led me to do yet another stupid thing. On the third day of our grief, I begged Ava, "Please never again. Don't ask me to go through this again."

She shook her head and replied, "Don't ask me that. I will want to hold and love another dog. Just not right now."

I knew that she was right, and I knew that it was erroneous of me to ask. People tell me I will change how I feel in time. No. I won't. I buried Pete over twenty years ago and though I spoke in the last few years of getting another dog—deep down I knew that I never would willingly open my heart to another dog.

That first week was horrible. In the subsequent weeks, the intensity of the pain faded somewhat but there was such a gap missing in our lives. Sydny was such a part of our daily routine. No greeting each time I came in the door. Naptime proved restless. The recliner we sat in for devotion was but an unoccupied piece of furniture.

It was two weeks after he left us when I drove into the Carolina Beach State Park to look at the sunset. It was still too soon. I don't even recall if I made it to the river to watch the sun magically bed down over the Cape Fear River as Sydny and I did so frequently. I was driving one moment and crying so hard the next that it proved difficult to see. I looked over at the empty seat. "Why, God? I am trying to understand. I prayed so hard over him. Why would you not allow us to have him a few more years? Did you forget what I asked of you? Ava had him for nine years before me. I wanted nine with him. I prayed this over him countless times and yet you chose to ignore my request. I just don't understand. Is he with you? I so want to believe that. This rainbow bridge thing—is it real or is it just something we foolishly cling to?"

The park that I once loved so much was sadly now a place of great lament. Occasionally, Ava went with us but for the most part—it was just Syd and me. Ava would still be at work and I would say, 'ride' to Sydny. He became so animated each time that I uttered that word, and he would start dancing eagerly toward the front door.

As dusk drew near it brought the deer out of the forest and they often stood by the side of the road. Sydny never knew quite what to think of them. He would stare silently at them with the most intense look etched on his face.

We walked back inside after Sydny was laid to rest. Ava asked if we could drive to the beach. There was a spot that she wanted to revisit. It was where I took her early in the morning the previous October 26th. It was the anniversary of our first date. I made coffee for us—the sun was barely up when I asked her to take a ride with me. She asked no questions, and she did not recall what the day symbolized.

We drove to the same spot and looked out at the ocean. It didn't help to ease our pain and I knew that it wouldn't, but you could not blame her for trying. I drove us back home a few minutes later. As we entered the house, she looked at me and touched my arm. "Thank you."

I shook my head—not comprehending.

"He loved you, Cole. He loved you as much as he did me. You gave him the best almost two years of his life. He was never happier than the time he spent living right here."

"Really?"

She touched my tears as she cried. "Yes. This was the best time of his life. Try to hang on to that in the days to come."

I still do.

5 ~ Petra

People and pets are filing through the gate as I began my ascent up the hill. It never becomes old watching the reactions of people. Some walk easily—soaking up the moment. Most look around in disbelief. Others raced down the hill when they recognized a loved one. My favorite is reserved for those who dance their way in.

I once inquired of Amos and later David as to the current age of my master. Neither knew and they would have not informed me if they did. David would rub my head and say, "Petra, none of us know these things. God does not want us to live for when someone is coming. He wants us to be thankful and rejoice where we are." Amos would just offer his patented look of disapproval along with the left head shake. I wish that David was my shepherd.

David once consoled me with loving pats on my rump and these thoughtful words. "I know that you are glad to be here, and I know you want to race up that hill and see Cole, but we have no way of knowing when that day will be." If I was a licker, I would have slobbered all over that dear man. But my master taught me long ago that was not desired. He would kiss me right on top of my nose and linger for a few moments—knowing that I would never lick him. I always wanted him to be pleased with me. He was frustrated often enough with his life. I strived to do all I could to make it better.

The people continued down the hill and the booms commenced. There is a firework display whenever a new group enters that makes any July 4th exhibit on earth look like sparklers in the back yard.

I remembered the information that Amos shared with me that I would need to know to help Sydney adjust to his new home. Typical Amos, being Amos, do you think he might have shared with me what Sydney looked like?

The fireworks ceased and the people and pets entered the village.

Color me confused. I looked for direction and not from Amos. In the central part of this paradise, there is the throne of God. We don't have or need sunshine here because the light derived from his majesty provides all that we need. While I am on the subject of living here I might as well clear up a few items for you. People work here. Everyone has a job but unlike on earth, there are no jerk bosses and people enjoy the tasks that they perform.

There are homes that people share with their loved ones. They retired to these places in the evening. The light fades but never leaves entirely during this quieter time—envision the most magnificent sunset or sunrise that you have ever seen and then multiply it a million times. That will not even begin to touch how picturesque it is. It is my favorite time. I long for the day my master is here to share it with me.

I gazed toward the throne and the most soothing warmth ran through my body. As I witnessed the majestic glow of radiance one lone ray divided and streamed right to me and as it touches me, I find that it tickles.

I am compelled to turn toward the hill once again. You have got to be kidding me. There is one small black Chihuahua mix, looking around sheepishly, unsure of what direction to take. There are only the two of us remaining on the hill. He hesitantly began his journey down the remainder of the hill. I waited for him—still in utter disbelief. I looked behind him once again. Peter was closing the gate. We don't call him Saint Peter here. We just refer to him as Peter. I have heard it said there has not been a big ego here since the evil one and those foolish enough to trust him were cast down. Why anyone could not be content here is beyond me. Now, I know that you are thinking about how much I miss my master and can't wait to see him. That is true, but even without him, this is a place is so wonderful it is indescribable.

"Petra?" This little dog is near me now.

"Sydny?"

His expression is one of incomprehension. I cleared it up for him. "Pets can communicate here."

He twitched his head— not comprehending that.

"Go ahead and ask me something, Sydny."

"Is this Heaven?"

I nodded my head, and I forged ahead and answered his next question before he can ask. "They are not here and don't ask anyone when or if they are coming."

"What do you mean if?"

"Everyone does not make it."

"They will."

I waited for his explanation. This should be good.

"I understand a lot more all of a sudden."

"That is because you have crossed over to what is referred to on the other side as *The Rainbow Bridge*. You will continually be aware of way more than you were on earth."

He laid down and stretched his front paws out straight and placed his small head between them. I still don't understand how my master wound up with a small dog, but he is a cute little guy. "Wait, you said they. Do you mean he has another dog?" I knew for certain it was not a cat. My master never had much use for them. He said they gave him the creeps.

"My mom," Sydny responded.

"My master is married?"

"Yes, and why do you refer to him as master?"

"It is what he was and still is to me. What do you call him?"

"Dad."

That ruffled my feathers a bit—I don't mind telling you. I didn't call him Dad. Sydny did not hear that. I am glad. Sometimes I communicate things that I don't want to be heard by anyone.

"You said they will come here. How do you know?"

"Mom and Dad love each other very much, but they love God as well. They begin each day reading the Bible and praying together. I sat in the recliner with Dad as he read each morning. It was one of my very favorite things to do. Do you think that they will be along shortly?"

I shook my head sternly.

He nodded—remembering he was not supposed to inquire about that event.

"How did you know it was me?"

Sydny's lip curled a bit. "There is a picture on the wall of their home of you. You are stretched out on the mountain top. The leaves behind you are gold. You are beautiful, and you look the same as you did in that picture."

I felt warm all over knowing that picture has traveled with my master for a long time. What Sydny said next surprised me.

"He would stop sometimes and look at that picture so intently and a sad smile would emerge. He would speak so softly. "Pete." Sydny lifted his head and said, "Pete, how does a beautiful girl like you wind up with a man's name?"

I think that my lip turned up with a smile. "We have a lot to talk about it, and the great thing is we have forever to do it. Let's walk down into the village." Sydny rose and we began walking easily.

I could tell that he was concerned about something. "Something on your mind, pup?"

"I hate thunderstorms, and I was hoping that there were none in Heaven."

I delicately took my paw and touched Sydny's head. "Those were not thunderstorms. There are fireworks set off when each group of people and pets make it here."

"I don't have to be afraid?"

"Not of anything." We continued to walk down the hill when I asked, "My master's wife—your mom. Is she beautiful and kind?"

Sydny looked at me and said, "She is the most beautiful and kind person that you could ever imagine." Sydny waited a little while and I think he knew my next question without my asking. "She loves your master very much, and she treats him like he is a king."

I was going to like this little guy. Ankle biter or not.

We heard our names being called. David walked briskly toward us—all of his little Chihuahua dogs in tow. Sydny snarled and the fur on his back spiked.

"There is no need for any of that. No one is challenging anyone. We all get along."

"Hello, David," I greeted the kindly man.

"David?" Sydny asked. "There is a picture of a David on the

fridge back home, but it doesn't look much like you. This man was a preacher, and my dad loved him very much. He talked of him often and even was toying with the idea of writing a book about the preacher and the bouncer. Whatever a bouncer might be."

David knelt and rubbed Sydny's head. "That is me, Sydny."

"I don't understand. You don't look like your picture."

"I was old then. There are no old people here—at least no one that looks old."

"What do I look like? I was eleven when I died and much of my color had turned to gray."

"You are black and brindle—with a little white on top of your head."

"Where is a mirror?"

David chuckled at that one. He rubbed his head again and said, "We don't have time here for pretense. No one stands on ceremony."

Sydny looked to me for clarification.

"No mirrors here, pup." He didn't understand but he would.

"Sydny, you can stay with us until your mom and dad arrive. We have a house that overlooks a large waterway. Your parents have land reserved for them across the street right on the ocean. You know your dad loves the ocean."

Sydny turned to me and I knew what his question was without his asking. "I don't live there. I could but I don't."

"Where is your house?"

"I don't have one," I replied.

He furrowed his brow—not understanding.

"Why don't you go with David? You will be fine."

David patted me on the head, and they walked on ahead of me. I turned back to the entrance, renewed with the hope that I would indeed see my master walking through those gates. I knew he would not be dancing. The man just does not have the rhythm for it.

I turned back around. Sydny was by me again. "I want to be with you. We have a lot to talk about. David said I can come anytime and that you would show me the way."

I looked down the hill. David smiled and waved. I have spent

45

a lot of time with him since he arrived here and sought me out. That is how I know that he is slightly disappointed that Sydny chose not to come home with him. The man could never have enough Chihuahuas to pet.

We begin our journey once again, down the hill, through the village, to the hill where I waited for my master. I wished there was a way to tell my master and his wife that Sydny is with me and that I will watch over him.

I had a million questions that I wanted to ask Sydny, but he was staring wide-eyed at all that surrounded us. I have stared at the gate so long in anticipation that sometimes I am sorry to say that I forget all the beauty that is present everywhere you look.

I didn't even mention how beautiful the buildings are in the village. Many are constructed with the most beautiful stone you can imagine. There are archways that were built millions of years ago, and they don't ever require maintenance.

Streets and walkways are constructed with stone. The main street, which sounds funny to me because streets are for driving and no one drives here, is made of gold pavers. That's right—gold pavers. How much do you think Home Depot would charge for those back on the other side?

I could be roaming through the lushest forests—running tirelessly on the hills—scaling to the top of snowcapped mountains without worry. There are lakes, oceans, and rivers I can swim in, but I do so very little of that as I stay perched on my hill not wanting to miss that first glimpse of my master.

Wildlife surrounded us. Deer and elk running free without danger of being shot—feeding off of the abundant grass that is present in endless supply. Bears, bison, sheep, wolves—you name it, though I am glad to say that I have seen no snakes. I don't much care for reptiles.

I am enjoying watching the little guy take all this in. You should have seen the look on his face when a mammoth Kodiak, grizzly bear waded through the sheep. He looked at me with wide eyes.

"The bear will harm no one."

He shook his head perplexed. It does take a little while to take all this in and realize Heaven is beyond anything that could be dreamed of on earth.

Midway up the hill, Amos waved at us. He grinned broadly. Another thing we don't have to do is shout at each other here. He chuckled and said, "I told you to watch after the *little* fella."

I don't bother to respond, and he is right in that is what he said. But come on, I took it as a figure of speech. Wouldn't you?

We made it to the top of the hill as the lights began to soften for evening. Sydny hunkered down low—burying his head between his paws. He looked up at me for reassurance.

"Will we be okay when it gets dark? I never stayed outside at night after Mom rescued me."

"There is nothing to fear. It doesn't ever get dark. This is just the end of the morning and people return to their homes. We have evening and morning. No night or afternoon. The sky will lessen some, but it will also begin to display the most vivid array of colors."

The little guy crawled on his belly toward me. He was still unsure. That was okay. I would watch after him. After all, he was my master's dog.

I laid down and watched the colors evolve. He was by me now, and he looked at me with a sad expression. He laid his little head on top of my front paws, and it was one of the cutest things I have ever witnessed. I placed my head on top of his small body. He was trembling slightly at first but soon I felt his body relax.

"Will we get cold?"

"Not here. Not ever. We don't get hot either."

"Dad will like that. He hates winter and cold weather. He only likes it at Christmas time and then he wants it gone for January. Lately, the winters seem to last longer or at least that is how he views it."

"He was not real fond of Christmas and after I died on Christmas Eve—I guess even more so."

"He loves Christmas."

I raised my head not believing what this surely mistaken pup had just communicated.

I could tell Sydny was amused at my reaction. "I believe that he is different in many ways since you last saw him."

"He complained about Christmas all the time. His anger toward God would start to build each year beginning near his birthday, in early November, and build through New Year's Day. The only time he enjoyed it at all was when he picked up Cody on Christmas afternoon and kept him till New Year's Day, but when he returned home after having to give that little boy back, he was always so despondent. There was little that I could do to cheer him up. It saddened me to see him that way. I would lay in the very back small bathroom off the master bedroom where we slept. It was as far away in that small house as I could get from him. I just could not stand to see him that way. It was also the place where I went to when he got mad. He occasionally would play a game with me where he would fake holler about a ball game on television or something, and I would just wag my tail, but when he grumbled under his breath, I hurriedly made my way to that tiny bathroom. It wasn't that I was afraid that he would hurt me. I just felt uneasy. He would calm down and come apologize and tell me it was okay and please come back to the living room with him."

Sydny raised his head and pawed me right in the spot on my chest that my master discovered was my favorite place to be scratched when I was just a puppy. I guess I had been going on quite a bit about my master's sadness and anger. It was apparent the little guy had something important to say.

"Petra, I don't know much about what went on back then during your time with him. He still gets aggravated, but it is always very short. He is happy. I may just be a dog, but I know that for certain, and he loves Christmas."

I shook my head in disbelief. Not that annoying left head shake that Amos does but a complete east to west shake of befuddlement. "How?" That was the best question I could come up with.

"God and my mom are the center of his life. He enjoys Christmas because he has someone that loves him to share the holidays."

"What if she leaves him?"

"I don't know about any other women, but he didn't have my mom. She is never going to abandon him. She would not tell him this but sometimes when it was just the two of us—she would tell me the only thing about Dad's age that concerned her is that he would probably come here first, and she did not think that she could bear life without him."

I thought about all this little guy was sharing. It sounded so wonderful and while I knew it was true—we don't lie in Heaven and for that matter it is not a good practice back on earth. God does not like it even a little bit. David once told me that one thing God loved the most about my master was that regardless his state of mind—God knew he would always get the truth from him. David also said it was one of his favorite things about my master as well. I know you think I am not supposed to be so knowledgeable for a dog concerning the things of God, but David tells me a lot and he is pretty far up the ladder when it comes to God. He is often included in meetings with Jesus and the apostles and Billy Graham and he often have coffee together.

The colors were becoming more brilliant now. There was the sound of worship throughout Heaven. Voices united as one.

Bless the Lord, O my soul
O my soul
Worship His holy name
Sing like never before
O my soul
I'll worship Your holy name
And on that day when my strength is failing
The end draws near and my time has come
Still my soul will sing Your praise unending
Ten thousand years and then forevermore

"She can sing as well."

"Excuse me, pup?"

"My mom. She brings down Heaven with her voice. That is what a worship leader once said." Sydny paused for a moment and then he said, "I know this song. It is one of Dad's favorites. The song is by a man named Matt Redman." He shook his head and said, "I can't believe how much I understand now. I mean dogs are way smarter than even their owners give them credit for but not like this."

49

He pawed the spot on my chest once again.

I looked down at the little guy that I was quickly becoming quite fond of.

"She will want to be your mom as well when she arrives." And you might not believe this and I would not blame you if you didn't but you know what that little guy did next? He winked at me with the most assured expression.

And I believed.

6 ~ Sydny

As we rested on the hill and relished the melting of colors into such splendor it is beyond depiction—I remained a little wary, but Petra has such a tranquility about her that it has helped to grant me solace. Her head nestled on top of my body sure does feel reassuring. I can hear a slight snore as she sleeps.

Back on earth, I think that I would have been jealous of Petra if she would have lived with us but now, I can't wait until we are all a family. Besides, how could anyone not love Petra? She is wise, kind, and I am so grateful that she is with me. I thought of David and while I sure do appreciate how he wanted me to live with his family—I think it best that I remain right here. As you might have noticed by now, I don't refer to her as Pete, the way Dad does. I don't know why, but somehow it just does not seem appropriate.

The colors changed slowly. I don't know how Pete sleeps through this, but I guess that she has been here for a long time. I still don't understand the concept of time but if Cody was a little guy during Pete's time on earth and a grown man in my time—it stands to reason that it has been a significant passage of time.

I bet Cody was upset about my departure as well. I would say dying but since I am more alive than ever it seems like an incorrect word. The first time he came home from Raleigh—I was the only one in the house. He opened the door and went straight to the bathroom, after which I refused to allow him to come out. How was I to know better? That was my home. It was my sworn duty to protect it. Cody had to call his dad to come home. Dad reassured me that it was okay and this was his son. Well, that was good enough for me.

I slept in his bed with him when he was home. He really enjoyed that, and I did as well. He is tender hearted just like his dad. I know he is shedding tears over my demise as well. Oh, that dang pit.

"No more about the pit, pup."

I rose easily—Pete's head rising off of my body. "Yes, I knew what you were thinking about. Don't ask me how all this communication works. I don't understand either. But the way I figure it is just like God wants people to just trust him—here and on earth. He desires the same for us."

The colors faded away as the skies became brighter. I watched as the atmosphere became the most magnificent shade of royal blue. "The sunset colors are gone, Petra?"

"Only to return, pup."

"This is beautiful as well."

There were stories that I heard back on earth that made little sense to me but right now they visit with such clarity. I have one for Petra that I just know she will enjoy.

"I have a story Dad often shared about you. Remember how you were talking about how he hated Christmas? Did you know his friends, Jackson and Kelly?"

"Yes. Jackson came to the house quite often that we lived in. In fact, he was there days before I left. My master hosted a Christmas lasagna dinner."

"Dad had a party the night before Mom and he got married. Jackson and Kelly were there and they spent the night. Cody was home, and he and I slept on the couch together. It was what Dad called a bachelor party. That is a party just for men but somehow Kelly was allowed to come as well but back to the story, and Dad told it that very night."

Pete stared intently—waiting for me to proceed.

"I hope I tell it accurately but it begins in a bar with Dad and Kelly. Neither one of them was in a festive mood about the holidays. I think that perhaps they had a little too much to drink but as the story was told they were sitting at the bar talking about how disappointing Christmas was. Now, this is the funny part that Dad told.

"He said, I hate Christmas. I got divorced at Christmas. I got unengaged at Christmas. My best dog died on Christmas Eve. And then he paused for several moments before dryly adding, Dang, I miss that dog.

"Kelly about fell off her stool she was laughing so hard. I am not sure why it was so funny. Maybe it was just Dad's timing that caught her off guard."

Petra nodded her head and replied, "I think I understand the laughter but also the true meaning of what my master was saying."

"What is the true meaning?"

"That in time the divorce did not pain him, nor did his broken engagement disturb him. The main part of the story was that he would always miss me and that I would be the one that remained in his heart forever. Thank you. That was a wonderful story." Pete paused for a moment before slyly adding, "I bet he didn't say dang either."

"I am new here but I kind of realize cursing might be frowned upon."

I heard a sound from some type of instrument playing. I had never heard anything like that before. Instinctively, I covered my ears.

"No sounds will hurt your ears here."

"Not even fire trucks and ambulances?"

"Nothing catches on fire and no one gets sick so we do not need such things," she said.

I see the source of the music. Amos has a twisted looking instrument in his hands that he is blowing into. I looked at Petra for an explanation.

"It is a shofar. It is made from a ram's horn."

"Is he trying to play music? It sure does not sound like much of a song."

"He is giving the call to eat."

Rising quickly, I ran swiftly toward Amos. There was a huge trough of food behind him. It was more food than I have ever seen in one place. And it looked like real food—not dog food. No complaints, the dog food was good that they served back home but there is nothing like people food. I wondered if there were eggs in it.

You are not going to believe what happened next. A dang red cat darted in front of me. I felt the hair rising on my back. I growled my warning, but it was really just a warm-up. It was on. This stupid cat was about to be chased into the next county.

That cat was so focused on getting to the food that I was on it in a heartbeat. I never actually caught up to one before. I was in unchartered territory, but my momentum took care of any concerns because I hit the hind end of that cat and it was startled so badly that it leaped over the trough. I ran around and began chasing that cat toward the woods that were off in the distance.

Now that horn was playing again, harshly, almost as a warning or command. I wondered who Amos was angry with. No worries. I have cat chasing duties. We were in the woods now. That cat was running for his life. The woods had the largest trees that I had ever seen, and there were beautiful wildflowers everywhere. There were manicured paths to walk on. Mom and Dad took me for walks in Carolina Beach State Park, but the paths were not this smooth, and sometimes I got a spur stuck in my paw. But this felt like walking on cushions. I stopped and looked around. I was in the middle of a dense forest. Everything was so fertile. There were waterfalls and crystal-clear creeks. I walked down to one of the creeks and saw a reflection of a dog behind me. Turning quickly, I saw that there was no one there. How could that be? I turned back to the water. Wait a minute. It was me in the reflection, and I didn't have any gray hairs. I wondered if you could drink the water? What the heck. I gave it a try though strangely I was not thirsty even after all that running. The water tasted better than the water back home, and my parents made sure that I had bottled water to drink. I know because I watched them pour it into my bowl. No tap water for this dog.

The beauty of the forest made me forget all about the dang cat. I saw a huge bear walking in one of the streams.

"We don't chase each other here unless it's for fun."

"That was fun."

He tightly shook his head as he looked beyond me. I turned and it was Petra. I was thinking that she would be pleased, but the look on her face quickly informed me that she was not.

"Don't do that again, Sydney."

"But it was a dang cat. Cats don't belong in Heaven."

"That is not for you to say. Some people love their cats as much as others love their dogs."

"No way," I replied. Surely Petra was jesting. Her stern counte-nance informed me that she was not.

"Cats in Heaven," I said. "Dad is going to be none too pleased about this." I paused, before adding, "Well, that cat was going to eat my food."

"It is not your food. It is for all the animals. Boy, did my master and his wife spoil you."

"Dine with cats?" I asked incredulously.

Petra shook her head. "Yes, and now we are going to walk to the food, which we will share with all the animals just as they share with us. You will not chase cats and do not eat like you are starving. Those days are behind us."

Boy was this a lot to take in at one time. Not getting hungry. Sharing food and worst of all—cats in Heaven. "Okay, Petra. I guess Amos was blowing that dang thing at me."

"Yes."

"Will he beat me?"

"Oh, good grief, pup. No one is beating anyone here. We are to be what people can't do on earth."

"And what is that?"

"Be kind to everyone and before you say it that includes cats."

"Will Dad understand that when he gets here?"

"Perhaps not but he will adjust as you will."

We walked through the forest back to the open area and toward the food. There was a howling noise as Amanda ran toward the food, hurriedly gobbling it up. It was the beagle that Dad had a painting of that hung on the wall back home.

I looked toward Petra for an explanation. "Amanda is a hard case. She is a work in progress and has been for quite some time. Amos almost whacked her with his staff one day."

"I thought you said no one hurt each other here."

"They don't. I said almost."

"Does she live with David?"

"No. She could never be a house dog. She just roams all around. She appears to be as self-centered as she was on earth." Petra sighed

55

heavily.

"Why the sigh?"

"Amanda was several years old when I came to my master's home. She never was very warm to me, except on rare occasions but for some reason, I loved her anyway. My master loved her also and he grieved terribly when she was hit by a car on Oleander Drive on a Friday night. I did as well."

Petra continued, "When we were outside, we had a metal building with two barrels full of bedding hay that we rested in or got in out of the weather. She died right before Thanksgiving, and I could not go in that building again.

"One rainy cold day soon after she died. I sat by the gate and watched the back door to the house. My master opened the door and instructed me to go into the shed. I did not comply."

"You sat there wet and cold?"

"I don't know why but that was easier than being in that shed with her seemingly all around but not really there."

"I don't understand."

"Neither did I."

"What happened?"

"My master came out and walked me into the shed. He told me to stay and then walked away back into the house."

"Did you stay in the shed?"

"No.

"Did Dad get mad?"

"He stood at the sliding door looking through the glass at me. He shook his head softly and then a look came over his face and I knew that he knew.

"He walked to me and opened the gate. We walked back toward the house, and he opened the door. Next, he picked me up in his arms and he felt me quivering from the cold and my fur being soaked.

"He began to cry, and he told me that he was sorry. He took me to the bathroom and gave me a long warm bath. He dried me off and then started a fire in the fireplace and laid my blanket beside it. I never was left in the back yard again that winter and by the next spring it was okay to be outside after my master cleaned every piece of dirt, dust, and straw out of that shed and put all new hay in."

"Outside living is harsh."

"Not really. There were certain times of the year that it was great. The yard was fenced in so no animals could get in, and I had no desire to get out."

"What about Amanda?"

"She could get out of anything. She never climbed much, but she could dig a tunnel across the country to escape."

We walked toward the food where I saw the somewhat stern look on Amos' face and believe it or not, I ate slowly for the first time in my life. Petra nodded at me once. I think she was proud of me.

Petra and I walked through the village after we dined with all the other animals, including cats. There was a blonde Chihuahua dog with their paws perched on the window sill. It is kind of funny that they call them windows because they have no glass in them. There is no need. I can tell you right now that annoying insects have not transitioned to the other side, and I think that it should be obvious by now that no one is going to break into your home, so there is no need for windows and doors that lock.

Mom is going to be thrilled that there are no cockroaches. She would scream like a serial killer was in the house when she spied one. It would startle Dad, and he would be perturbed with her but only for a moment. He would walk to the origin of the cry and kill it. She was so grateful you would have thought the man had slayed a dragon. I don't know why I just said dragon because I don't even know what one is. Must have been something I overheard from Mom and Dad.

I walked toward the dog in the window and cocked my head a little to the side. Dad always thought it was one of my cuter looks.

"Sydny," the dog perched on the window sill said.

"Savanna," I whispered in stunned amazement.

It was Mom's dog that she had when she got me. Savanna was older, and I remember how sad Mom was when she had to have her put to sleep. I sure am glad that she had me to help her through that time.

The door opened and a lady welcomed me inside. There was a little boy with curly blonde hair holding her hand. I noticed movement behind them. It was a black and white cat. I almost took off after it but then I remembered that I am not to chase cats.

"Hello, Sydney. My name is Amber, and we have been waiting for you."

That was strange since I did not know that I was coming here. I looked back through the door where Petra still stood. She nodded her head and then she continued her walk.

Amber closed the door and smiled warmly at me. She was beautiful and her eyes were so captivating. They were a deep royal blue color, and it seemed as if they were bottomless pools of water. She had long, lustrous, thick brown hair.

She sat on the floor and motioned for me to sit in her lap and I did so. The little boy stood behind her with his hands on her shoulders. He was a curious little fellow. Savanna came over and nuzzled me. "It is so good to see you, but I am sorry that you had to leave Mom. Did she have another dog as she had you when I passed away to help her through it?"

I shook my head no.

"Oh. I hate the thought of her being alone."

"But she is not alone," I remarked and then I began to share with them about the wonder that is my dad and her husband. The glow on Amber's face was so joyous that it appeared to fill the Heavens and if you have not grasped it by now this is a rather vast place.

"I'm sorry, Sydney that I was not nicer to you. I was older and in a lot of pain— the truth is that I did not want to share Mom with anyone. I took it out on you. You probably did not even like me."

I shook my head firmly in disagreement. "I missed you when you left. Mom began to put my bowl where yours once rested. It just did not seem right so I would not go near it. Mom figured it out and returned my bowl to the regular place." I thought of Petra at that moment and how she grieved over Amanda and refused to go back in her house even if it meant sitting in the cold rain.

I had not noticed until now just how big this house is. Correction, I am pretty sure that this would classify as a mansion. There was a winding staircase that seemed to ascend forever. It was then that I noticed that where the first level of steps ends there was a platform full of little children. I looked higher, and there were three more similar levels, and they were all are filled with these wonderful smiling children. Doggone if there was not a tabby cat walking along the banister.

Amber explained to me that this was a house of healing and that there were many such homes as this. Somehow, I understood that Amber took care of all these children and that they were youngsters who were lost, orphaned, or abused so badly that they lost their lives before it had hardly begun. She serves as the good parent that most likely they never had on the other side. They would never carry memories of not being wanted. They would know nothing but love. And in that moment, I understood that Heaven could not be perfect —void of the warm laughter and innocence of little children.

Amber motioned for the children to come and see me. They descended down the steps and were all over me—petting and tickling me, as they joyously giggled. You will probably find this hard to believe from a once very ornery dog, but I enjoyed it so much that I did not even think about nipping them—not even once. They were so infectious in their happiness and even though they stumbled so close to me it is amazing that none of them stepped on me—but this is Heaven and even if they had, I am pretty certain it would not have brought injury to me.

Later, after all the children went back upstairs, Savanna and I sat in Amber's lap in the most comfortable recliner you could imagine. I told them about Petra and her vigilant watch for her master, my dad. Amber had a lot of questions about Dad.

"He is hard on himself and thinks he always comes up short, especially when it comes to Mom." I shook my head gently. "But if you could see the way she smiles at him—you would know to never ask another question about how he treats her. Mom often said to him that he made her feel as if she was the most beautiful woman in the world."

The most satisfying smile enveloped her face. "That is all I need to know. Thank you, Sydney."

"Mom talked about you often to Dad and many times she voiced how much you would have loved him. Mom misses you so much."

Amber shook her head tightly and gently, and I saw tears escape from those gorgeous eyes of hers. I knew they were good tears.

I did not realize that I had spent almost the entire day here at this wonderful home until I saw the pink light drift through the window. "I need to return home."

"You could stay here," Amber said hopefully. "Not just for the evening but until your mom or dad comes," she added.

"I won't leave Petra alone on that hill."

"But no one is alone here."

I just shook my head and nuzzled Savanna. "I will visit often." Savanna placed her cheek on mine.

Amber opened the door for me. Even in Heaven, I did not know how to open a door. I turned back and looked inside. The children were all grouped around Amber and waving excitedly to me. Amber smiled and said, "I am so glad that Ava is happy and has someone special to love her. No one ever deserved it more."

I walked through the village and toward the hill. Now before you start to think that I am perfect because of this being Heaven—you are going to be disappointed when I inform you that I got a little lost. I walked up one hill—certain to find Petra only to see a herd of cattle—where a Border Collie and an Australian Cattle Dog were keeping them together. Frustrated, I walked back down the hill and of course, I ran into Amos.

He looked away from the sheep and pointed diagonally to the hill. "That is the way, Sydney."

I walked up the hill and was relieved to see Petra sitting and watching the gate as it opened and another passel of people and pets entered their forever home. The music drifted toward us and the warm feeling that enveloped me was beyond words. The sky more colorful than any painting you could imagine. The combination of sunrise and sunset colors that were afresh each time

"You could have stayed with them, pup."

"I know," I answered, as I stretched my paws across her legs and tucked my head between them. She laid her head ever so gently down on top of mine. I think she was glad that I kept choosing to remain with her.

7 ~ David

The light in the sky brightened, and I looked forward to the task at hand. I nodded to Sara and informed her that I was leaving. We don't say goodbye in Heaven, and we also don't have to worry about our loved ones being hurt or any of the uncertainties that consume much of our time on earth.

Stepping outside from our home—I stopped and admired the beauty of the geraniums that are on each side of the path that leads to our door. They were my favorite flower at our home at Wrightsville Beach. They are here as well. I particularly loved the ones with blooms that are such a vivid color of cobalt.

One of my favorite things to do here is gardening. There were too many things that interfered with the pleasure that I derived from digging in the dirt in my time on earth. Especially, during my many years—serving as a senior pastor.

Cole assisted me with landscape projects when I retired and unfortunately aged. Being older was going okay and there was much that I could still do, but an errant driver veered into us on the highway one day and my health was never the same. I know some people questioned God that if someone like me, whatever that means, is not protected, how could they ever feel secure. I was frustrated with my decline in my physical being but to query God was not something I was inclined to do. He had proven far too gracious to me.

Sometimes Cole brought Cody to help out when he was just a little guy. I once asked if I could give Cody ten dollars for his help—knowing full well that Cole would never take a penny from me for his labor.

Cole was respectful to me as he always was. "No," he said with a slight shake of his head. "I want him to know what it is like to help people and ask for nothing in return, and thank you for asking me first."

I don't know why I bothered to even try. My response was, "I had a feeling that would be what you would say."

If I would have given the money to Cody without permission Cole would have granted me grace and not corrected my interfering. He was not much on granting leeway to authority. Preachers were no different. He also didn't budge in regards to his father but then their relationship was never much of anything to write home about. They were as different as night and day. I was his spiritual father. We never used that term but some things you just know, but the word that best summed up our relationship is friend. We were friends and it was evident that it was very special to each of us.

I walked along the waterway and admired the beauty of the open waters. I loved my spectacular view at our home in Wrightsville Beach but it is quieter here. Allow me to clarify that point. There seems to be worship music playing at any time, but it is always so peaceful that it just filters in with everything else. It is like one big harmony.

I gazed back at the cottage that my wife Sara and I live in. It takes me back to the first place we lived here. It was a mansion like the Bible spoke of. Jesus was quite pleased with what I had done on earth, but eventually, I respectfully asked for something smaller. I was just a simple preacher that loved people and tried my best to encourage them. I am grateful that Jesus found that I did it well. You never forget that first moment when you enter this place. Jesus and King David, my favorite Biblical character, greeted me with hugs. Jesus spoke first. "Well done good and faithful servant." You can't ask for much more than that after nearly nine decades spent on earth. King David smiled and said, "A man after God's own heart."

The newness of this place never wears off. No one is ever bored because we all have this peace that can only be gained in slivers of time back on earth. Here it is as constant as the waters flowing around the rocks of our many waterfalls.

I continued up the hill toward Petra and Sydny. I left my Chihuahua dogs home because I wanted this time to be with the two dogs my friend loved so much. Besides, I would be home before evening to sit in the easy chair and do one of my favorite things both here and on earth. Pet my little Chihuahua dogs.

Petra saw me first and lifted her head and wagged her tail. Sydny stood beside Petra as I dropped to my knees. They loved on me as I petted them.

"Sydny, how are you adjusting to your new life?"

"It is a nice place," he answered in slight understatement, dropping his head slightly.

"They will be here when the time is right. I assume that Petra has enjoyed the updates you have given her about Cole." Petra pawed at me with her answer.

"I have told her all about my mom."

"Cole's mom and I sure prayed for a long time about this woman. We were pleased to see how beautiful inside and out Ava is."

"But how could you know that? You were gone before they met."

"There are balconies here and on occasion, some of us are allowed to look over the edge and see certain events that the Lord deems right for us. We don't see ugly things because then it would not be Heaven so much, right Sydny?"

"I guess so. Tell me more about seeing my mom."

"I was allowed to be a guest of the wedding." He chuckled and added, "They just did not have to feed me, though the food sure looked good. I was allowed to listen to some of the toasts given.

When Cody gave his toast there was not a dry eye in the house, especially from Cole. He loves that boy, but you guys knew that already." He paused to rub their heads before continuing. "The minister, James, who conducted the service was not only an associate pastor on my staff, but he was also like a son to me. At the first prayer, he spoke of Cole and my relationship. Cole began to cry. Petra, I want you to know that Sydny's mom wiped those tears away with such compassion that it brought me to tears. We don't have sorrow here, but we do sometimes have good tears. It was easy to see that they shared a special kind of love and they always will. Even when they arrive here."

"Will Dad be first since he is older?" Sydny asked.

I smiled at Sydny.

"I'm sorry."

"It's okay and understandable. I felt that way often when I arrived and my wife Sara remained behind. But what is important for people to remember is that God should have always been first with us and not our spouse or children, or anything else. Why don't we take a walk in the woods?"

Both dogs quickly joined me. One on each side. We walked to the edge of the forest where tulips and bulbs bloomed profusely. We are not limited to seasons and plants that briefly bloom. Picture a plant at its peak and that is how it is all of the time, except better.

We entered into the woods. Sydny stopped to look up at an ascending hill that was filled with trees of varying heights. There were waterfalls that flowed into different shapes and sizes of pools. Beautiful stone benches and lanterns were scattered throughout. We were in the Japanese Maple Garden. There was a myriad of specimens with different shapes, leaves, and bark colors. There were varieties from the very early days of creation that no longer existed in the world. All of the trees proved stunning in appearance and flawlessly landscaped.

"They look somewhat familiar to you, right Sydny?"

"We have similar trees in the yard back home but not this beautiful."

"We had two of them when I lived with my master in our home as well," Petra added.

"One thing has not changed and never will in regards to Cole. Japanese Maples are his favorite tree—his favorite plant."

We stopped in front of a tall, skinny waterfall that was so high that it seemed to emanate out of the sky. At one point the waterfall quickly divided around a huge boulder into two streams. It flowed in this manner until it was twelve feet from the bottom, at which point the two streams merged into one before entering the pool below. The pool of water was bordered on each side by various types of weeping Japanese Maples. Several feet above the pool—on a little parcel of flat ground was a bench, constructed from ancient wood.

"Petra, walk to the bench. Sydny, you go with her."

The two marvelous creatures eyed me curiously—not understanding my request.

I nodded gently.

They walked the short, curved trail, and stopped in front of the bench. They both turned to me with puzzled expression. "There is reading on the bench, but I don't know what to make of it," Petra conveyed.

Oh, I was enjoying this because I did not see writing at all. In a moment neither would they. "Turn back to the bench," I suggested.

There was a picture on the backrest of the bench of Cole and Ava. Both dogs began to bark. Moments later the image faded back to words.

Sydny whimpered softly. I navigated the brief walk and sat on the bench. I patted each side of the wood beside me. They both jumped on the bench and laid their head in my lap.

Sydny looked up at me with his dark, kind, thoughtful eyes. "What does all this mean?"

"This is a unique place created for Ava and Cole."

"Because my master loves waterfalls?" Petra inquired.

"Partly."

"And the other parts?"

"The water that continuously runs to this pool contains all of the tears that Cole and Ava have ever shed. The sad ones. The tormented ones. The lonely ones. The happy ones. This bench waits for them. They will spend much time here enjoying the soft fall of the water—the beauty of the Japanese Maples. Knowing Cole, he will want to jump in the pool of water, and Ava will go with him because she would follow him anywhere."

"Wow," Sydny said.

"May we go in the water?" Petra asked.

"Certainly," I answered with a hearty laugh.

Petra waded in as Sydny looked at me apprehensively. "Go ahead. Nothing to fear, remember?"

He jumped down and waded into the pool. They enjoyed the water so much. At one point, Sydny climbed on Petra's back and laid down as Petra swam slowly in circles.

They relished the water for what might have passed as hours back on the rushed other side. I sat and marveled at the goodness of God. They walked out of the pool and jumped back on the bench beside me. I rubbed their wet bodies.

"Make sure you don't mess up that bench before they arrive."

We all turned to the sound of the voice. Standing in the path was a short man with a red shirt and a blue hat with WP written on it. He held a dark blue mug of coffee. We could see the steam rising from it. He had a mischievous slight grin etched upon his face.

"I am certain that you know that nothing can be impaired here. So, your interest in this bench is because?" I inquired.

"I built it," he answered with a slight grin.

"Do you know the people you built it for?"

"One of them for certain. I am glad that he found a woman worth sharing such a well-constructed bench. "Good to see you again, Petra girl." The man tipped his cap and walked away.

Sydny and I looked at Petra for an explanation. She seemed uncertain but then clarity emerged in her eyes. "That was Buddy. Dad's brother-in-law."

"That's right," Sydny chimed in. "There was a picture on the wall back home of him. Dad talked about him frequently, particularly if he was doing a project that involved woodworking. He would get exasperated, and I would hear him say, "Buddy, please give me some guidance. Now it all makes sense."

We felt such joy at all that had occurred around this special pool. A pool created for two people that would forever enjoy walks in the woods—quiet time, and play in this inexplicable place.

Later, we rose and strolled quietly through the forest. There was wildlife all around us. I watched in slight amusement as Sydny realized that there was no need to be afraid. Wolves and lambs were walking together as if they knew no other way. Birds filled many of the trees, and there is no need for them to migrate. I thought of the scripture of how not one sparrow falls to the ground without our Father's knowledge. That verse is not about the sparrow as much as it portrays the depth of love that he has for us. Sadly, more than any other thing back on earth that has distorted the image of God is religion. How we must carry out written rules while making sure we refrained from doing bad. People can get so caught up in performance issues that they lose sight of the primary focus, which is about having a relationship with our loving Father. The closer that we live with him as the center of our lives—the less we need written rules.

"I met with Jesus recently, and I asked him for something that I hope is all right with the two of you."

Sydny cocked his head, inquisitive about my next words, while Petra continued walking easily in her calm manner, but I knew she was listening. She always was. I have grown very fond of her. I wish she would stay at our home, but her fierce loyalty to her master did not subside when she passed through to this side.

"I am now your shepherd."

"Not Amos?" Petra asked.

I shook my head.

"Did he take the news badly?"

"Not at all. They put him in charge of a thousand more sheep. It is more in his comfort zone."

That is good since the sheep have that much more value than us," Sydny thoughtfully shared.

"It is not that way at all," I responded.

Petra spoke next. "We had so little value to our life when we were born and then we found our way to someone who loved us. I guess people often feel that way when they are born into a family that does not want them."

Such insight from this beautiful creature.

We continued our stroll in silence. We stopped at a pool that was fed by a waterfall that climbed up a majestic steep mountain. The water cascaded down upon the most beautiful rock formations. Ducks and geese swam effortlessly in the pool. Fish swam near the surface in the faultless water.

"I don't understand why people would discard us the way they did," Sydny said sadly.

"Money, and sometimes people just don't want to be bothered but turning an animal out in the cold is a terrible act. But what is important for both of you to understand is that even though you were un-wanted originally—remember to reflect upon the value you had to Cole and Ava. Let's sit here," I said, gesturing toward the bench to the left of the trail that was placed in front of a field of radiant golden wildflowers that stretched out as far as we could see.

I sat in the middle of the bench. Petra jumped up to my right. Sydney looked at me, and I knew that he wanted to be in my lap. He could have jumped up, but I think that he just wanted me to pick him up. I knelt to gather him and he circled several times just out of my reach before moving in cautiously. I picked him up gently, and he nestled in my lap. I rubbed his head and said, "It will not hurt to be picked up any longer. The pit is gone forever."

He looked at me and then he laid his head into my stomach. "I want to tell you a story about value as it pertained to you back on your time on earth. Petra, your dad bought a house before he was ready. Sure, he knew he should for Cody's sake. Still, he would have waited another year or so but he wanted you with him. His only regret was that it turned out to be only for four years.

"And Sydney, he spent two thousand dollars trying to save you when in his heart he knew that you weren't going to make it. Not bad for a seventy-five-dollar dog."

"Will they be okay without me?" Sydney asked.

"Not right away," I answered, rubbing his shiny coat thoroughly.

He stretched his paws out in front of him and buried his head between his paws. "Don't they know that I will be here with Petra waiting on them?"

"They will want to believe."

"Why won't they?"

"Back on earth, there is a poem called *The Rainbow Bridge*. It is about how our pets come here to wait on us but there is nothing that I could ever find in the Bible to substantiate it. Your mom will believe it more than your dad."

"Because she loves me more?"

"No. Not at all. Your dad just does not accept things as a certainty just because they sound good. He always desired the truth, regardless of whether it is good or bad."

"So, the rainbow bridge has no meaning and Dad will think he has seen the last of me?"

"I did not say that."

"Well, what did you say, and is there a way God could show him so he won't hurt so badly?"

I shook my head in slight dismay. This little guy sure was persistent. "He desires that Cole walk by faith."

"But you just said the rainbow bridge is not biblical."

This little guy actually made me squirm. I did not know what to say. Me, a preacher, with no words. That would certainly bring some chuckles back on the other side.

The same bear that Sydny had seen previously walked toward us. He approached and with his massive paw, reached out to Sydny. Sydny burrowed into my stomach trying to disappear.

It was Petra who spoke next. "Ben won't hurt you. Nothing is going to ever hurt you again. Not a pit. Not a human. Not an animal or sickness."

Sydny turned to face the massive animal. "Ben?" He was also startled because he was pretty sure that Ben spoke out loud. Could some animals here actually speak audibly?

"Yes," Ben said, as he delicately rubbed Sydny's head. Smiling softly, he said, "No more chasing cats."

Sydny could not believe it. He liked this talking bear. "I only wish the grizzly bears back home were friendly, especially now that I am not there to protect my parents."

Sydny thought of a story and he began to share. "It was the middle of the night, and I knew something was at our door. I have never done anything like that before, but I jumped out of my bed and charged that door—barking and growling the entire time.

"Dad got up to see what was happening. He stood by me as I eyed that door. He walked toward that door as I continued to let that intruder know what would happen if they tried to hurt my mom or dad.

"He flipped the switch to the porch light and peered out the window. I hated what he did next, but he made me stay while he opened the door and walked outside to inspect what was happening.

"I was so relieved when he walked back inside, though I had not stopped growling for one moment. He knelt on the floor and rubbed me and told me what a good boy I was. There was nothing good about what I was doing. They were mine and I don't care if that grizzly bear was trying to get in or not. He was not getting to my humans if I could help it.

"After that he put me in their bed. I always loved that. It was one of my favorite things. Dad would most times go to bed before Mom did. I would sleep with him till Mom came to bed and when she would try to pick me up to put me in my bed, I would cling to Dad. She would chuckle but she still placed me in my bed as she kissed my face a dozen times. That woman was a kisser."

Ben asked, "Why did you mention grizzly bears?"

"Dad was often saying, *Flick says he saw some grizzly bears near Pulaski's candy store!* I thought it might have been a grizzly bear at the door that night."

I chuckled softly. "That was a joke. That is a line that is in the movie "A Christmas Story" about the little boy that wants the Red Ryder BB gun."

"That was a joke?"

"You were a brave dog for charging who or whatever was at the door but there are no grizzly bears at Carolina Beach."

Sydny shook his head. "I might bite Dad's ankle when I see him." But he didn't mean it.

Ben petted Sydny one last time and then said to Petra, "You are beautiful as always sweet girl." The friendly bear sauntered away far more gracefully than you might expect of an animal weighing close to half a ton.

8 ~ Cole

Ava and I had planned a vacation months before we lost Sydny. It was our plan as it was anytime that we went away to leave him with Ava's parents, Don and Jan. They have two older dogs of their own, Dachshunds, Charlie and Ginger.

It was the last day of October as we drove away from our home at Carolina Beach, through the city of Wilmington, and we were now at the northern end of New Hanover County, where the road turned to Interstate 40.

I looked over at my wife who was settling in her seat with numerous things near her to read as we make our way to a cabin in a little place, called Dugspur, Virginia. It is located in the southern mountains of Virginia—near the Blue Ridge Parkway. One day, I would like to drive the entire Parkway without a timetable. There was a time when a much younger man dreamed of hiking the Appalachian Trail but age, surgeries, and my preference for warm showers has removed that one from my bucket list.

We neared the exit to Castle Hayne where her parents resided. Sadness enveloped Ava's face. Often during these last thirty-four days—I have been in one room and suddenly I would hear wailing emanating from the next room. It broke my heart each time. Sometimes, I went to her and tried to help and other times I ventured outside—unable to take her tears.

I reached over and took her hand. Sometimes a story about Sydny helps, and I decided to go that route now. "Remember the last time we went to the mountains?"

She nodded softly and a few tears leaked down her face. She wiped them away hastily for fear of ruining her makeup. I always complain about how long it takes her to get ready, but the results are always worth it.

The last time we left Sydny with her parents was earlier this year. We went to Hanging Rock State Park for a weekend. I backed my truck out of their drive that morning, and Sydny stood just inside the front door of their home peering out worriedly through their full-length glass storm door. He never liked to be left behind.

Don't get me wrong. He loved Ava's parents. He would settle in and be fine, but when we returned to pick him up the joy in that dog's heart was something to behold. I guess in dog time—being away a few days translates to at least one year.

I did not realize a lone tear from my thoughts trailed slowly down my cheek. Ava missed nothing when it came to my heart. I felt her hand gracefully wipe it away. "Tell me the story," she requested. She has made similar requests often, and I know that she will continue to do so. I think she worries that she might lose a single wonderful memory of Sydny. Right after he was gone, she would often start a question with, "Remember how Sydny use to?"

I began the story. It showed at the time how much he had grown into my heart. It was late in the afternoon and the image of him gazing out of that door as we drove away remained with me. I called my mother-in-law when we got settled in our cabin.

"How is Sydny doing?"

"He has spent most the day staring out the door at the driveway," she responded. "He is either there or right next to me."

I often wondered how these rescue dogs that come from such horrible beginnings always know. Regardless of age they never seem to lose the fear of abandonment or the gratitude of a loving home where mealtime is not hit or miss. That image of that little guy staring through the glass door was one of the most forlorn things that I have ever witnessed.

"Remember the first time that you came to the apartment?"

My wife's question shook me from my thoughts. I nodded my head. It was her turn to tell a story that she has shared countless times.

"I was so nervous about you meeting Sydny. I prayed and prayed that my little dog would love the man that I was already falling in love with and that you would love him in return. Sydny never liked men except for my dad and that took time. He was wary of everyone but especially men. I'm certain that his abuse derived from the hand of men.

"But he was such a smart little guy. I guess that somehow, he knew that you were a good man and would be around for the long haul. You sat nervously in the recliner that now rests in our home. You did just as I instructed. Allowed him to come to you. You sat down and he immediately jumped in your lap—turned his back end toward you and looked at me. After a few minutes, you began to nervously pet him but you would not put your hand near his face. You just kept stroking him from the middle of his back to his hind end. I don't think that he moved once the entire time that you were there."

We rode in silence for several miles, and Ava sorted through some magazines she had brought and pulled out some typewritten pages. I couldn't imagine what they would be as any work stuff was off limits.

My thoughts drifted to my favorite story about Sydny. I was working part-time when we were dating. It helped supplement my pension but boy was it a boring job. I took two weeks off during the holidays that year and since Ava was still working most of the days—I suggested that she leave Sydny with me. She was driving to my house almost every evening after her workday. That way she could just come straight to my house with no worries about taking care of Sydny and as a bonus I would have dinner prepared.

As early January arrived, I suggested that with our schedules and Sydny being alone in the apartment for much of the day—why not let him just stay with me. We had already secretly decided that we were getting married in April anyway.

She was not that crazy about my idea initially, but she was glad that I offered, and she liked the idea of him not being alone so much. I think her parents helped her with this when she told them about my suggestion. They said it would be good for both of us. I didn't know what that meant at the time.

He stayed with me for the first two weeks of January before she took him home one night because he had an appointment with the vet the following morning. I always smiled at the picture of what this little guy did. He laid on her bed for two days—save going to the potty and to eat. The remainder of the time he stayed on her bed and pouted. Her roommate at the time noticed it and said to Ava, "Sydny is pouting. Do you think it is because he misses Cole?"

Ava grimly nodded her head and thought there was one sure way to find out. She drove to Carolina Beach after work, and he remained in the down position with a sad face right up until the moment she drove into my neighborhood and then he rose from his sulking and began to bark and wag his tail.

I was not expecting her visit when the doorbell rang that night. Sydny walked in first and did a happy dance. He was home. I can still hear the clicking noise his nails made as he danced on the hardwood floors. She shook her head and told me the story. I couldn't help but grin. She demanded that I stop, but she only meant it a little.

He never spent another night in that apartment, and we were becoming bonded at the hip. I had let my guard down and allowed another dog to take up residence in my heart.

She was settling in her seat and began earnestly to read whatever was in those typewritten pages.

"What are you reading?"

"I found a short story that you wrote about Petra."

"Why would you want to read that?"

She touched my hand and smiled tenderly. "Always trying to understand my husband."

"Is it that difficult?"

"Sometimes yes and sometimes no.

"I did not think that you wrote short stories," she added. She knew that I had several manuscripts laying around the house from long ago.

"That is not a short story. I pulled it out of a long, horribly written manuscript. It was the first thing I wrote and at the time I thought I had a story but as time passed and I would reread it I realized that while it had some interesting things the flow in the story was lacking."

"Why did you pull it out of that story?"

"I thought one time about submitting it as a short story to build up some credibility when I pitched other manuscripts."

"Did you?"

"No."

She squinted her eyes in slight disapproval. "You can't expect to be published if your stories remain stuck in a box in the closet. How are you going to write us out of poverty with the next best seller if you don't submit the books?"

I smiled at our inside joke. Whenever she would interrupt me when I was writing, I would jokingly say, "I am trying to write us out of poverty, dear."

"Now, be quiet and allow me to read about this dog who you loved above all others."

I nodded and asked her to play Third Day on my iPod. Settling in to drive—I relaxed and watched the miles drift away to the soothing sound of the powerful voice of Mac Powell as Ava began to read.

Pete
(CHRISTMAS EVE)

I parked my black Wrangler Jeep in the driveway, in front of the older modest brick ranch that served as home. Entering the house, I walked down the hall to my bedroom. I heard a muffled grunt from the small bathroom in the corner. Pete was letting me know that she was trying to sleep. It always amazes me how a dog can take thirty naps a day, and even then, it is not enough.

"Get up, old girl," I said, as I bent to pat her on the rump. I probably should explain why a female dog is named Pete. It was originally Petra and the name naturally got consolidated over time. She is eleven years old and beautiful once again. The summer heat was hard on her, and she had contracted heartworms that nearly killed her, but now she has regained at least fifteen pounds bringing her weight to just over fifty, which is about normal. I suddenly recalled seeing ornaments scattered under the Christmas tree in the living room. I feigned being upset. "You've been drinking from the Christmas stand again, haven't you?"

She lifted her head from the worn, white tile, looking as innocent as possible. I don't understand her infatuation with drinking water that is for the Christmas tree, but she frequently ignored her clean water in the kitchen to partake in it. Maybe it is her seasonal version of eggnog.

Often, when I heard the slurping, I forgot the ramifications and called out hastily to her to stop. Inevitability, upon hearing my voice she would turn quickly to escape and dang near bring the tree down with her. Since I wasn't here to catch her—it was only a couple of ornaments this time. Most dogs wag their tail. Pete shakes her whole rump. If she is near a wall when it happens you would think that the house was caving in. I held her chin in my hand. She stared softly into my eyes—her tail thumping the floor gently. "No more drinking from the Christmas tree," I demanded firmly. Softly she growled and sighed deeply as if to tell me that I am boring her. She laid back down and immediately resumed snoring. Nap number thirty-one is a work in process.

Later that night I dropped mom off at the house I was raised in. I had taken her to church for the Christmas Eve service. It was my first visit to church this year. I had fallen a long way from my born-again conversion that occurred many years ago.

The loneliness of the holidays seems amplified at the moment, and I chose to delay entering the emptiness of my house. I drove to Wrightsville Beach. Approaching the archaic drawbridge—the stationary rails were adorned with white lights. It is hard to view a bridge that backed traffic up forever during the warmer months, as boats glided underneath it on the Intracoastal Waterway as pretty but I try.

I crossed over the bridge and saw the live oak trees along the highway medians clothed in white lights. Side streets adorned with candles glowing inside plastic jugs, lighting the way for Santa. The road void of vehicles. Christmas Eve night—the second loneliest night of the year—only surpassed by the emptiness of Christmas night.

I drove the loop and finally spotted an automobile. It was a lone patrol car. People are home with their families as they should be, or even with a girlfriend. I don't have that either. I think of a girl I loved long ago before I was married. It was the one time in my life I was in love and I was too young, too immature, and too full of myself to appreciate it or her. Her name was Paula and I wondered at times such as this if I will ever truly love again.

I leave the Island behind and all the lights that failed to brighten up Christmas for me on this night. I come to grips with a thought that has long been with me. Maybe love like I felt with Paula was a once in a lifetime *experience.*

I do not know if it is my way of saying goodbye to a dream, but I find myself taking a slight detour on the way home. I am driving on Airlie Road—the town's most scenic drive. It was just off of the Island. The Intracoastal Waterway is on my left and lines of mature live oak trees adorn the right side.

I entered the private driveway of Paula's old neighborhood. It is a loop road and I expected the area inside of the loop to be the always beautiful natural area with gigantic gnarled live oaks that I recall. The original developers had promised that it would remain in a natural state but as I reached the beginning of the loop, I see homes constructed where the massive trees once stood. I shook my head at progress.

I continued my slow drive until subconsciously stopping in front of Paula's old house. The house appeared the same, but the landscape around it has swelled. The light of the moon nestled in the top of the massive live oak tree that towered over the house from the backyard. The backyard that I could not see now except in the visions that flowed peacefully through my mind. The St. Augustine grass with blades so thick and plush that it felt as if you were walking on air. The slope of the back yard ran gently down—meeting the natural grasses that bordered Bradley Creek. I could picture the vast view. The coastal landscape that stretched on endlessly—best enjoyed from the upper balcony.

I could see the inside of the house now. The game room on the first floor, where we sat to get away from her parents. The stairs led to the kitchen, where I could almost hear the housekeeper, Annie Mae, saying, "Cole, can I cook you something to eat? You know that I don't mind." Annie Mae was a dear sweet soul.

The outside light flashed on— waking me from my dreamlike state.

The door opened abruptly and a man peered out at the intruder in front of his house. I drove away slowly.

I headed for home and reminded myself that at least on this night I would not be alone. Pete would be there to greet me.

Minutes later, I was standing in my driveway. Pete had slipped away just before I had to leave to pick Mom up for church. She never went far and typically just visited a few neighbors in hopes of deriving a snack from them, which she often did.

I comforted myself that in the morning she would be in the bushes by the front door. I opened the door and could not shake the nagging feeling that something was wrong.

I got back in my jeep, backed out of the driveway, and drove to the stop sign. I turned left and drove slowly to the next block. My heart seized when I saw the big black ball of fur lying motionless on the grassy shoulder, underneath a substantial sycamore tree.

Stopping the jeep, I walked to the front of it and slumped back on it. "Pete," I called softly, knowing better. The tears came quickly. "Thank you, God, for our time together," I muttered.

I bent and touched her fur. She was still warm. There was not a mark on her. A clean hit by a car, a heart attack—I would never know for sure. It didn't matter. She was gone. Perhaps, if I would not have taken my trip down memory lane, I would have been here in time to get her home to safety or if I would have insisted on finding her before I departed to pick Mom up for church. Add both to my lengthy list of guilty memories that haunted me nearly every day of my life.

Her favorite blanket was in the back of my jeep. I slipped it under her, gently cradling her as if she was still alive. Gingerly I lifted her, placing her on the floorboard.

I rested my head in her fur, covering her with my tears. "I do not know if dogs go to Heaven, but if they do, surely you are there."

The courtyard was dark except for the dim moonlight that filtered through the tall pine trees. Slowly, I made my way through the short trail in the woods, carrying my faithful companion. She was buried by candlelight in a plant bed in front of the deck.

I stood for several minutes over the freshly covered grave. I gazed up to the sky that was lit up with a million stars. "Seriously God. Christmas Eve night," I stated with weary exasperation. "I have to pretend that all is well tomorrow and not ruin Christmas for the family, especially Cody. You know how good I am at pretending," I added sarcastically. Breathing deeply, I shook my head in dismay. Looking down at the grave, I said, "Goodbye, Pete."

We were drawing closer to Raleigh when my wife put the papers away.

"Discover anything new about your husband?"

"That you thought you might never find love again."

"But I did," I answered softly.

"You most certainly did," she softly said, before laying the seat back and closing her eyes. I heard a slight snore within moments. I was always fascinated by her ability to fall asleep so quickly. I drank in her splendor and silently thanked God yet again for choosing me to show her just how truly beautiful she was.

9 ~ Sydny

Petra walked me through the most magnificent mountains one day. I know we don't have days, nights, and time here, but I don't know another way to describe it for you. The thought of a little dog like me scaling mountains thousands of feet high gave me pause, but Petra just nodded and I knew that it would be okay.

There are waterfalls everywhere and I know Dad will love that. I heard him say to Mom that waterfalls were his favorite part of the mountains when they were planning their honeymoon.

I wanted to go on the honeymoon as well but even as self-centered as I was, I kind of understood their desire to be alone. It was almost worth the absence when they returned to take me home. I was so excited. Grandma Jan opened the door, and I ran circles around them until I exhausted myself and then they loved on me in such a wonderful way. I am certain that they missed me as much as I missed them.

"Have you ever been to the mountains, Petra? I mean back on the other side."

She merely nodded, and I could tell by her twinkling eyes that it was a pleasant memory.

"Did you like them?"

"Not as much as just being with my master. He would brag about what a great traveling dog I was and how he would point to the floorboard on the passenger side of his jeep. I would curl up and stay right there until he told me otherwise, regardless of the miles that passed by. I was just glad to be with him."

"What was your favorite time with him?"

"I just told you."

"Going to the mountains?"

"No. Just being with him. The destination mattered not."

"What about a favorite part of your daily life with him?"

Petra's eyes sparkled once again. "It was the way I woke him in the early morning when I needed to go outside. I would rest my nose right on his face. One time he sensed me approaching and before I could touch him, he quickly raised his head and kissed me right on top of my snout." She paused, before asking, "What about you Sydny? I know that you loved the sunset rides to the park but what else?"

"Sometimes, especially at night, Dad would open the back door and let me out to do my business. There was a fenced-in patio so I could not get away. I would come back to the door and bark to signal to them that I was ready to come back inside. He would stand at the door and act surprised to see me. Often, he would turn to Mom and say, there is a little bitty old doggie at our back door as he was opening the door. Where did you come from? What's your story? Did you travel far? Would you like a little *sumpin* to eat? That is how he would say it. I think he made the word *sumpin* up. Mom loved it when he did that. Her favorite part was when he would say, did you travel far? I would act annoyed but deep down I loved it, and I always got a treat for coming back inside."

We climbed to the very top of the mountain and looked out over the landscape. You could see forever. The villages were filled with people. The pasture lands complete with animals. Wild horses roamed freely. I think I even saw Ben walking with a den of bears that were different sizes and colors, as well as other Kodiak bears like him.

This communication thing stretches a long way here because all of a sudden Ben stood on his hind legs and waved toward us. I barked and though it sounded a normal bark to me—I knew that he heard me.

Petra laid down and surveyed the entire splendor both above and below. "Thank you, Petra for taking me in. I know I could have stayed with David and been happy. I understand everyone here is happy. Still…"

"We are family."

We laid there and both of us fell asleep. When we woke, evening was upon us. I love that it is never dark here. It makes sense though when you think about it. Even a little dog like me understands that God is all about light.

We watched Peter open the gate for the next wave of new people and pets. A beagle was sitting near him.

"Yes, that is Amanda. She likes to hang out with Peter, and he seems to enjoy her company as well. I heard David explain it one time. He said they were both free spirits, especially on the other side, so they naturally gravitated towards each other."

I lowered my head and scratched by my right ear. I probably should have mentioned this by now, and you probably have already surmised without my informing you, but there are no fleas here. Occasionally, I scratch—not because of an itch but more just from habit.

"What can you tell me about their wedding, Sydny?"

I gave a slight growl that was not a snarl but an agitated clearance of my throat. "I am still a little upset that I was not allowed to go. It kind of hurt my feelings, but they came back that afternoon and I was with them. They were so happy. Mom was so gorgeous. She wore an elegant gray dress but what was the most stunning was the glow on her face. Your master could not be loved more by any other woman."

I looked down the hill, and there was Amos—rod in one hand and staff in the other. He pointed toward the village. I followed his direction and when I looked, I saw David with two women. David was beckoning to us to join them. The vision you have here is simply amazing. No need for eyeglasses or contacts.

We walked down the hill toward David and the two ladies. The two beautiful women stood tall and strong. I walked toward them and sniffed their ankles. I know people call little dogs like me ankle biters, but I just sniff people out of habit. I am a dog and that is what we do, even in Heaven.

They both knelt and begin to love on me and after a few moments, it dawned on me who they were. "Dad's mom and grandmother."

They both smiled warmly. I knew at that moment the exact right thing to say. "He carries you in his heart every day."

Dad's grandmother bent and scooped me up in her arms. "I am your great grandmother, Sydny."

"May I refer to you as grandma like my master still does?"

She laughed heartily. "Yes, you may certainly do that," she answered as she placed me back down on the abundant grass.

"He worshipped the ground you two walked on. I am not exactly certain what that means, but I sure heard him say it often."

They nodded gratefully.

Cody's grandmother picked me up and kissed me right on top of my snout. "Can I call you Mimi like Cody did?"

She hugged me tightly and responded, "I would like that very much."

I nuzzled my head into her chest. "I don't understand it all, but I know that you had been sick for a long time and that you came here soon after Mom and Dad got married. Dad knew you were home, but he still grieved greatly when you passed away. One morning in particular he was so shattered and I remembered Mom holding him and saying repeatedly, 'You are not broken.' I don't know exactly what all that meant." I paused for a moment before adding, "And I did all that I could for him as well. God created dogs with this instinct to know when their humans need them the most. I would lie on his chest and face him with my front paws stretched out and my head buried between them. Dad loved for me to do that. He would rub me gently, and I could feel some of his worries depart. I know you want to see him again, but he is in the best of hands with my mom."

Grandma spoke firmly, "Good, I would not want to have to get a hold of her."

I think she was joking, but she sure had a stern expression on her face. I think I understand something Dad told Mom once. That his grandmother was his protector when he was little.

"Let's walk to the balcony," David suggested. We began our journey to yet another place in this marvelous kingdom. It might just take eternity to see it all.

We walked through the village until we approached an extensive set of twisting steps that stretched into the sky as far you could see. There was a chain crafted from gold below the first step and a guard standing in front of it.

"David," the guard said warmly. "I was told you were coming with a party of four." He unclasped the chain and motioned with his hand for us to proceed up the stairs. We walked past him and I heard the chain click back to its previous position. "Don't fall off the edge," he warned.

I looked to Petra seeking reassurance.

"Nothing to fear. He was joking."

"Have you been here before?"

"No, pup."

I sighed deeply. "Pup is not my name. I am tired of being called that. Everyone else calls me by my name. Why don't you? I don't even shorten your name to Pete like Dad did. Please reciprocate."

She chuckled and placed her head on top of mine and said, "Okay, Sydny. But you will always be my little brother," before adding, "Reciprocate. That is some fancy language for a dog."

I felt kind of bad for snapping at her. It was really the guard's fault for frightening me. Perhaps I will nip one of his ankles on the way back.

We continued our ascent up the stairs. Stairs that appeared to be made of glass and shined our reflection back to us. I am glad that Petra has never been here previously. We can discover this treasure together. There were more stairs than I could calculate if indeed I could count. My language may have escalated greatly, but my math skills remain limited. We reached our destination and sat in the most restful chairs that you have ever relaxed in. We looked below and all I could see was the sky. That did not make sense. The sky is above us.

David as usual explained everything where we could all understand. "People often mention about peering over the balcony of heaven? It really does exist. Right now, you see the top of the skies, and we are prevented from seeing earth. We can only see it if Father opens the sky to allow us to see something he knows will be beneficial for us. You can imagine he would not want us up here all the time watching what goes on back there."

"Because then it would not be Heaven, right?" I asked.

He rubbed my head tenderly. "That is exactly right."

"Are we going to see something down there today?"

"No," he responded with a shake of his head.

"Why are we here then?" I retorted curtly

"Patience," David answered. He was quiet for several moments and then he said, "I was allowed to watch the wedding that you missed out on."

I still had not learned yet to limit my questions about people that made it or did not make it to this wonderful palace. "Why is Cole's dad not with us? Did he not make it here? Was he allowed to watch the wedding?"

David looked at me with a somber expression and slowly shook his head.

"I know. I know. I ask too many questions or at least the wrong ones. You can't blame me for being curious."

David smiled and rubbed my head once again. "He is here and I don't know who was permitted to see the wedding. Heaven has numerous balconies."

David said softly, "Speaking of Bill. Cole's dad. Right now, he is probably sitting in the fire station. He is happy to be there. Lots of firefighters here."

David began to laugh and then he said, "They even have a fire truck in the station, even though we know there will never be a need for it. Speaking of the fire truck, Bill decided one day that it would be a good idea to see if the siren worked. Remember how that went over, Beatrice?"

Cole's mom shook her head tightly in dismay.

"The siren did indeed work," he said with a chuckle. "And once he turned it on it got hung up. None of them could shut it down. It kept getting louder or maybe it just seemed that way and became more annoying the longer it was on. Finally, Haywood, one of the firefighters figured out how to cut it off."

David chuckled once again before continuing. "James, the brother of Jesus, went and had a little talk with Bill and the other firefighters. He told them if they wanted to keep the truck that better not occur again. Bill learned his lesson though he still likes to tell the story."

I kept looking down, hoping that God would open a window, and we could see below. I so wanted to see Mom and Dad. Looking around I noticed everyone but David was also peering below. He caught my gaze and smiled, nodding his head. He knew what I was hoping for.

"Look straight ahead," David instructed.

We did as he directed, and this gigantic movie screen appeared. There was a group of people on the beach. I got so excited when I saw that one of them was Dad that I barked and everyone laughed. They were not laughing at me. We don't do that here. We laugh with people, but we never try to hurt people's feelings. I bet God wishes it were that way on earth. Imagine if people spent more time trying to encourage each other rather than tearing each other down. Dad said once that the reason people ridiculed others was so that they could feel like they stood a little taller. Dad wasn't like that. I think he knew what it was like to be the underdog. He had a heart for those that got made fun of. He got picked on a lot when he was little. He never told me that, but you can just add that to the plethora of things I have learned here. Like using the word plethora.

I watched the scene on the beach. There was a young guy playing guitar and then I saw Mom walking down a wooden walkway toward steps that would lead her down to the beach and to the people who were waiting.

I pawed Petra's chest. "That is my mom."

"She is beautiful," Petra responded.

"In so many ways," I answered with a small sigh.

We sat without additional conversation and watched the wedding on the beach. I know you won't believe this, but we were served popcorn by these two nice ladies. Only in Heaven. All the popcorn you can eat and you don't even get a belly ache.

10 ~ Petra

The video of the wedding had pleased me greatly. I never witnessed my master looking so happy and peaceful at the same time. The expression on his face as he watched Ava stroll down that walkway. I am so happy my master is in such good hands. I look forward to meeting her one day.

I sensed movement below, and I can't help but laugh. It is Ben and Sydny. Ben has taken quite a liking to the little guy. He will saunter up here on occasion and ask me if it is all right if Sydny takes a walk with him. A more polite bear you will not find.

They were at the edge of one of the many forests here when Ben turned to wave. Sydny rose on his hind legs and performed a little pitter-pat with his front paws toward me. I barked softly. They withdrew into the forest. Only in Heaven could a bear and a mixed Chihuahua become the best of friends.

I sensed movement below and turned my eyes to see a haze of light moving in my direction. There was a silhouette amid the light and then the cloud of light vanished. I saw a man walking toward me. I know, however, that this is not just a man. My skin tingled and warmth engulfed my body.

"Petra, what a wonderfully loyal dog you are. You sit here patiently each day waiting on your master."

"Jesus?" I asked sheepishly.

He nodded softly. Wow! The Lord has come to visit a throwaway dog like me. Who would ever believe such a thing?

I wish I could describe exactly how he appears. The reason I can't is because I can't stop looking into his eyes. They appear to be a shade of blue that I am not familiar with but what sets them apart is they are so translucent it is like looking into one of the lakes here where you can see to the bottom. We don't have pollution, so you can't even believe what our lakes, rivers, and oceans look like. Each one is crystal clear. I know my master loves the ocean back home, but he has not seen anything like this. The best aspect of his eyes is that I have never perceived such tenderness. As I continued to look at him in amazement—he sat and began to pet me. I contemplated if anyone on the other side would believe that the Son of God took time to pet a dog like me.

"Do you know that they talk about you down in the village?" he asked.

"You mean the dog that does not have the good sense to accept repeated invitations to live in a home with others?"

"Is that what you think they say?"

"Is that why you are here? You are going to make me leave this hill and live with someone in their home," I say resolutely.

He continued to pet me in silence. I wondered if I have overstepped my bounds by my remarks.

"You have been very kind to Sydny. He was unsure when he first arrived. You have welcomed him and taught him well. Best of all you have taught not by words but by example. I could use a lot more humans like you back in the world."

He rose to his feet and began to walk back down the hill. He had only managed a few steps when he turned and there was a smile on his face that matched the warmth of his eyes. "The people in the village say that you have supreme loyalty that is unmatched. They speak of you in terms of complete admiration." He paused for a moment as I drank in his words. "I have a task for you to complete."

"What is it, Lord? I will do whatever you ask—even if it means I have to leave this hill."

He laughed heartily. "Quite the opposite, Petra. You are to remain right here on this hill and watch the gate each time the trumpet sounds, signaling that another party is arriving. You will stay here until your master enters."

"I wanted him to come soon but now after hearing all that Sydny has shared about the love between Ava and my master, I realize how much she would miss him."

"Why do you think that your master will come first?"

"Sydny informed me that my master is several years older than her. I know that she could come first but she probably won't."

"Yes, he is her Boaz." He smiled kindly and said, "She never once worried about their age difference, but your master did to the point where it not only got on her nerves but mine as well."

"You don't have nerves, Lord. Is that what people call a figure of speech?"

He chuckled with amusement. "That is a valid point. How about you allow me to worry about Cole and Ava?"

"But you are the Lord. You don't worry."

He laughed so jovially that I noticed the people in the village below gazing up in our direction. His laughter fills all of Heaven and then I heard laughter everywhere. It echoed from the villages—the forests— the mountains and I can hear through all the laughter a little bark and I know without question it is my little friend, Sydny. I wish he was present to witness this visit.

"I have one more request for you, Petra. Come visit anytime and bring Sydny with you. Just walk to the light." And then he was gone and I don't mean he walked down the hill. He vanished. I shook my head at the magnitude of what had just occurred.

I recalled something Dad said once about his idea of Heaven. You never have to say bye to anyone that you love.

11 ~ Sydny

Petra snored slightly. Of course, you know by now if you have been paying attention that no one gets tired here—sleep or no sleep. That will be good for Dad because I know that he suffered with insomnia during our time together.

Sometimes, when he struggled to fall asleep—he would wake me as he picked me up out of my little bed. I did not like being awakened, but he would take me to the big bed and place me between Mom and him. Sometimes, as he rubbed me it would calm his mind enough so that he could fall asleep. I was glad to help.

"Deep thoughts, Sydny?" Petra inquired.

I did not answer her question.

"You are thinking about my master."

It was not a question. Petra, the wise girl that she is, already knew.

I waited for several moments before speaking. "How old do you think Mom and Dad are now? We have seen a lot of evenings from this hill, but I have no idea how long I have been here."

"That is by design as you well know."

"Do you have any idea how long it has been?" I persisted.

Petra answered with a slight shake of her head.

"Do you think that they got another dog?"

"I would think so. Dog lovers do that."

"I know Mom would desire to but Dad—I am not so certain that he would choose to have another dog."

"What makes you say that?"

"The way he talked about you. He never loved another dog till I came along. We bonded in such a way. I wish our time would have not been cut so short." I paused and breathed deeply. "I also wish there was a way he could know that we are here waiting on him."

"Maybe he knows."

"Perhaps," I answered without conviction.

It was the first light of morning as David approached. "Sydny, you have questions that the Lord has sent me to answer. Follow me," he instructed. I stood and walked to him. He looked back at Petra and patted his hip gently. She rose and joined us.

We walked back to the steps that led to the balcony where we viewed Mom and Dad's wedding. The same man was standing just below the first step. Has he been here the entire time? I speculated as to whether they pay overtime in Heaven. You know I am just teasing you. There is no need for money or possessions.

"Party of three this morning, Shepherd," he said, addressing David, as he unhooked the chain. He petted Petra and me for a moment and then waved us on our way. We were a few steps up when he said, "Remember, don't fall off the edge."

I turned back to him, and he was grinning broadly. I gave him a courtesy bark to inform him that I have grown in knowledge since my previous visit.

We sat in the front row of the balcony and waited for David to speak. Worship music played. David lifted his hands upwards and sang along with the peaceful song.

How can I say thanks
for the things You have done for me?
Things so undeserved,
yet You gave to prove Your love for me;
the voices of a million angels could not express my gratitude.
All that I am and ever hope to be,
I owe it all to Thee.
To God be the glory, to God be the glory,
to God be the glory
for the things He has done.

"Who sings all these songs?" Petra asked.

"Different people and worship teams. There is always a song of worship being sung somewhere in Heaven." He sighed deeply before continuing, "And unlike churches, no one is quarreling about the type of music that they think should be played. A church can be so divided over the style of music and that is why many are forced to have two types of services. Traditional and contemporary. I guess that is okay but the end result is often two different churches underneath one roof. I am glad I don't have to deal with those issues any longer."

He paused and looked at Petra. "That particular song was sung today by Andrae Crouch. It was a song he wrote during his time on the other side."

"Does anyone make new songs here?" Petra inquired.

"Absolutely, and writers like your master write new books."

"Wow," I said. "That is so cool. Are we going to be able to look below?"

He nodded and my excitement grew. Petra wagged her tail furiously. I bet you could hear the thumping throughout Heaven.

I smelled popcorn, and this time it was delivered by an angel. I love this place. We still can't grip things with our paws, but we don't stick our head down in the bucket like savages either. I don't know how this works but when we desired a piece of popcorn—it floated up to our lips and we just opened our mouth and sheer deliciousness ensued.

"Sydney, before we begin the viewing, you asked Petra if your parents got another dog."

I scrunched my face and looked at Petra.

She merely shook her head. "I didn't tell but you should know there are no secrets here."

"There are none on the other side either," David said. "People only think they can hide things. God sees all."

"So did they get another dog?"

"Yes and no."

"What? You either have a dog or you don't," I replied, somewhat perturbed.

"You know your mom wanted another dog in time. Your dad didn't. He said after you passed that he would never bury another dog, but as you well know he never could say no to your mom. So, he relented in time and your mom went with her mom and picked out a black and tan Chihuahua mix."

"Like me?" I responded.

"There is no dog like you or like Petra for that matter, but he was a sweet dog."

"Wait. You said, yes and no. Do they have a dog or not?"

"They did."

"The dog died?"

He gazed at me with a blank expression, and I knew that I was asking too many questions but doggonit I could not help myself. "I don't understand," I said, shaking my head.

"The dog lived with them for several months. Your mom loved the little guy…" he said, his voice trailing off.

"But Dad was not nice to the dog?"

"You know better than that. He treated the dog fine. He just refused to open his heart. He knew there would come a day like it did with Petra and you, and he would have to dig a hole and place you in the ground. The pain was too powerful. Petra, he still has the most vivid dreams about you, and you have been here for a long time."

"How long?" Petra asked.

"Nice try," he answered quickly.

"What happened to the dog? I bet they gave it to Mom's parents. They would take it in."

At that precise moment the top of the sky opened and we could see below. "Mom," I barked furiously. She was older but still oh so beautiful. She was on some type of farm, and she was feeding all these animals. Dogs, chickens, goats and horses.

"They can't hear you, Sydny."

I kept barking anyway. There was a big weathered barn and a man walked slowly out. "My master," Petra cried out.

We watched as Dad walked toward Mom as she was removing something from the paw of a red Australian Cattle Dog. Dad approached her and sensing his presence, she looked up and smiled. She patted the dog, and we could hear her say, "You are okay. Go play."

The dog scurried away, and Mom grinned widely as she hugged Dad. She kissed him on the lips just like I had seen her do a thousand times. It warmed me all over that they were still this way toward each other.

96

Dad was older, and his gait was stifled a bit, and I knew that the pain in his left leg had not left him. His hair was grayer and his blue eyes still twinkled with tenderness as he looked at Mom.

David said softly, "Sydny, when I prayed for a woman for your dad I did well, didn't I?" He chuckled faintly at his rhetorical question.

I almost teased him by saying that ministers ought not to be wearing their hands out patting themselves on the back, but I just quietly drank in the sight of Mom and Dad. Just as Petra was. We even forgot about eating popcorn.

"What is this place?" Petra inquired.

"Your dad said several times that if he ever received a substantial six-figure check from writing that he would drive to the place your mom worked and bring her home. She would be by his side."

"I remember that. He also said he would fill a huge Tupperware container with those dental chews I loved. So, he got the six-figure check, and Mom works here?"

"No, he received a seven-figure check the very week that she took the dog to her parents. A film company in Atlanta was told about his book, *The River Hideaway*, and they bought the film rights and hired your dad as a consultant. He bought this place with some of the money, and your mom runs it primarily as a shelter for abused and unwanted animals. Some get placed in homes after she thoroughly checks them out but if no suitable homes are found they remain here," he said pointing below. "Back to my yes and no response. No, they don't have a dog at home, but she loves every animal here. Your dad loves them as well, but it is just easier for him to love them here and not in their home where they become part of so many daily routines."

David watched the two dogs—their faces in complete adoration at the people below. "Go ahead and bark again."

I looked at Petra. We were both confused, but we complied and barked for several moments. Our tails were wagging, and I knew that my oversized ears were spiked high.

Cole and Ava looked around curiously. Ava even looked toward us, but she was not allowed to see. They both had a puzzled expression etched on their face.

Ava turned to her husband. "For a moment I thought I heard Sydney bark."

"I thought I heard that and Pete as well." He shook his head not understanding.

The screen began to close and when it was fully closed and only the top of the sky was visible. I climbed into David's lap and nestled against him. "Thank you."

He petted me, and I felt Petra's headrest on top of my little body once again. It was a group hug.

12 ~ Cole

The doctor's office called a few minutes ago. The news was not good. I had a cancer scare last year. It was colon cancer and twelve treatments of chemo produced a subsequent clear scan.

Ava was by my side every step of the way as I knew she would be. I never deserved Ava—I tell this to God all the time, but I tell him with complete gratitude that he chose otherwise.

I am driving north to a place between Rocky Point and Burgaw where I was able to purchase the land for my wife to rescue every animal she could. I have been blessed beyond measure. There is no mistaking that. My writing career took off after *The River Hideaway* was turned into a major film. I was determined that it would not change us, and I think we have been true to that. We still reside in the same house in Carolina Beach. We thought about moving but then we decided to convert the single car garage into a double with a nice spacious room over it. It serves as our exercise room, and there is a small office in the corner of it where I write.

People think I am nuts because after the film deal, I was besieged by literary agents who wanted to represent me. Ironically, it was many of the same ones who had rejected my work previously. I chose to work with my attorney and close friend, Wylene, who meticulously combed over each contract I was offered. She offered solid advice and often got me more money than was originally offered, but my main reason for choosing her was that I knew her and I trusted her. Maybe, as I have been often told, I left millions on the table, but how much money do you really need? I wanted our lives to remain simple and never lose sight of what is significant.

I also refused to sign multi-book deals. I never wanted to be forced into a situation where I had to write a book to fulfill a contractual obligation or just for the money. We took the film money, and we did some things for others and ourselves. The things we did for others we did our best that no one would know but God. That was not always feasible, but we did press upon those we helped that they were to tell no one. Good deeds should be done discreetly. The praise of people I could care less about—just as I do not care about critics who deem my work too spiritual or simple. Well, you can shoot me right now if that is my offense because I am both spiritual and simple, and I am in complete comfort with those facts.

A wise man that I bought Cody's first bicycle from once said, "The more stuff you have. The more headaches you have keeping up with it." I don't like headaches.

We did have a modest log cabin constructed in Sparta, North Carolina. There is a small creek that runs through the front yard and occasionally, I tried my hand at fly fishing. My dear friend, Bryan Daughtry, met me there when we first bought the place, and he taught me how to fly fish. It sure not as easy as they made it look in the film, "A River Runs Through It," but occasionally, I was able to catch dinner for Ava and me.

The creek runs so near to our cabin that when the windows are open you can hear the sweet sounds of the waters as it moves. One of my favorite things in this life is being able to sit by the creek and read from the Bible in the morning and books of fiction in the late afternoon.

Ava and I stayed at the cabin often, and we rang in the New Year there for several years and remained there till spring. Many years I wrote my first draft of my next novel in the solitude of the mountains during that period. Ava balked the first few years we did this because she did not want to be away from her animals for that long, but she learned that the people we employed were quite capable of caring for them in her absence. Still, most years she insisted on driving home to check things out at least once. She always told me that I could stay and write and that she was quite capable of driving alone—I never allowed that. She is my baby, and I am her protector. I know I am old fashioned, but she doesn't seem to mind.

Aw, back to the doctor's phone call. The cancer has returned, and it has spread. I am told chemo may extend my time, but it is highly unlikely that it will eradicate all the cancerous cells. I feel pretty good for now, and I want to enjoy life here for as long as possible. The doctor gave me the news and then passed the remainder of the call to the scheduling coordinator to schedule my chemo sessions. I ended the call before she came on the line.

She called within minutes, and I informed her that I would not be doing chemo. Not again. I knew Ava would not be happy about me making this decision alone—as we decided all the important matters in our life together—but not even she could dissuade me from the course that I know I will not deter from.

Leaving her behind is what I feared from the day we fell in love which was within the first week we dated. We knew as unlikely as it appeared that we were the right fit for each other. I am not saying God spends his days playing matchmaker, but he sure let us know that he would be with us if our paths became one. Still, it was our choice. We both had suffered our share of pain and risking your heart can prove a daunting path to venture down. We could have chosen to cling to our fears, but we risked sharing a life together, and the rewards we have enjoyed have been beyond our wildest dreams.

Some of our first dates were about sharing our wounds and a wonderful thing began to occur. We not only fell deeply in love with each other, but our love began to heal the hurt of our past.

One of Ava's favorite things to share about those first few weeks was how I would share these gut-wrenching things about myself. Finally, one day she held my face in her hands and looked into my eyes, and stated firmly, "You keep saying these things as if that is going to be the one thing that persuades me to walk out the door. I am not going anywhere. I am here to stay."

There are no words sufficient enough to state what that meant to me. I won't even try. She would not be another woman who would say, "I can't live out of my heart the way you do," before departing.

We celebrated our twentieth anniversary last month in early April. Perhaps, I will make it to the twenty-first but not the twenty-second. I do admire people like my parents who were married for just shy of sixty years, but I have no regrets. We made a vow as entered marriage that what we would never achieve in quantity—we would make up for

101

in quality. We have done that.

I turned off the main road onto a gravel road that leads to the rescue farm. I am a little stiff as I get out of the truck to open the aluminum gate where our property begins. There is a sign to my right that reads, *Ava's Farm—Where animals come to be loved.*

The gravel road winds through the woods, and there is a mass of trees flush with new growth. Pines, oaks of different varieties, maples, sycamores, cherry trees—all planted by God. We keep the underbrush cut back so that there are trails for walking and riding horses.

The land opened up and the farm was upon me. There were several barns, and the one closest also contained an office where Ava kept up with paperwork.

Naturally, during a time like this, I reflected on Heaven. I never say who might make it or who won't. There are enough judging Christians in this world. It is like they skip over Matthew 7:2. *For in the same way you judge others, you will be judged, and with the measure you use, it will be measured to you.*

Still, I have to tell you that people that abused animals, especially dogs—I think they might be in trouble when their time comes to appear before God. There was a time I wondered if I would make it. I had the big Damascus Road experience of my youth, but I fell away and cursed God often for his so-called plan.

Later in my life and months before I met Ava my anger subsided and one day as I drove the streets of Wilmington and before you say it—I know how cliché this will sound. But trust me this is how it occurred.

As I gripped the wheel, I said softly to God. "*I am so tired of doing it my way. Everything I have touched has failed. Whatever path it is you want me to walk I will follow. I will let go of what I think I have to have. I don't want to be alone forever, but I also don't want to be involved in any more relationships that you do not approve of. Besides, if you are not in the relationship—it will fail just like the ones that preceded it.*

I always have this image when I reflected upon that time of our Father, saying to those around him. "Okay, I have his attention. Let's go to work."

I met Ava a few months later on the first day of July when she barged across the front of church to introduce herself. I had no idea that she had noticed me one day when I was pumping fuel in my vehicle at our local Costco. She was in the car with her parents. A few weeks later she felt led to return to the church she once was a member of that also just happened to be where I was attending church.

We did not begin to date right after that first contact. We talked but while I sensed an interest on her part, I could not get past our age difference. I would mention getting together for coffee, and she readily agreed to that, but I did not follow through until that fall.

We met at a park. I had picked up coffee for us. We ran out of coffee but not conversation. Three hours passed and we went to lunch. Seven hours after meeting that morning for coffee we finally went our separate ways. As I drove home to Carolina Beach, I was apprehensive as I asked, "God is this it?"

I tease her to this day about how hard to get she played. As we were parting that day she said, "If you ever want to do this again, please call me." By the time I made it home she had sent me a text that read— this was the best day I have had in a long time.

It was for me as well, and we were inseparable from that day forward.

We were married the following April on the beach. She was the right woman to hold my heart through the good and the bad times. In a few short years, *The River* Hideaway—the story that I wrote the first rough draft of nearly sixteen years prior was published by a small press. The dream of the right woman and to be a traditionally published author granted by God. The very dreams that I thought I might be giving up to follow him.

I told God often that I did not want to be a published author for fame or fortune. My biggest desire was to witness someone reading my book on the beach and enjoying it the way I have enjoyed reading the works of so many fine authors. Another dream was that my book might be under Christmas trees at some point. We had a second book signing the year my book was published at the local Barnes & Noble. The second one took place two weeks before Christmas. Most of the customers that day had read *The River Hideaway*, and they loved it and bought multiple copies for Christmas presents. I signed dozens of books that day, *Merry Christmas*. And even though I would not be there to witness it on Christmas morning—I knew my books were scattered under Christmas trees from here to the state of Washington.

I parked the truck and shut the engine off. "Father, how do I tell Ava that I must leave her behind? She once asked me to never go where she could not go. And now I am going to do just that.

"I know you have a plan but right now this is a plan I do not desire. I don't even know what to ask of you. I have lived a good life but if you wanted to heal me and extend it a few more years that would be good. No, that would be great.

"Somehow, I know that is not the plan. I ask that you walk through this with us hand in hand. I am not worried about myself. I know that you wait for me on the other side. I will see Mom, Grandma, and David among many others. I wonder Lord if Sydney and Pete are there. You never answered my request to show me that sign after I buried Sydney to assure me that he was there. I have discovered nothing scripturally to substantiate such a thing.

"But what is most important now is that you have to take care of my wife. Grant me this last request."

I got out of my truck and walked through the office area looking for my wife to share the news that would shatter her heart. I prayed that I was man enough for the task.

13 ~ David

As I sat on the porch watching the water as majestic skies part-ed and God's light came forth to begin another sequence of our endless time here in Heaven. The spirit of God rested upon me. "Please come to the throne."

One of the great things in this life is we live continually in the su-pernatural. It does not come and go as it did on earth. Sometimes, back on the other side, there would be such a long pause between supernatu-ral events that it was enough to cause even a minister to doubt.

"Did you hear that, David?"

I gazed at my beautiful wife. She was left behind when I came here ahead of her. I wondered why I thought of that at this particular time. I nodded my answer to her.

"Well, don't you think you better be going?"

"Why? Do you think that I will be late?"

"Oh, David," she said with an annoyed shake of her head. "Just go. Our Father has called."

I sensed someone at the door. Turning, I saw Paul, who wrote a large part of the New Testament. This must be important.

I walked outside, and we began our journey. "Is it one of my sons or grandchildren?"

Paul shook his head. "Do you know what your wife, Sara, said to Cole at your visitation?"

I shook my head.

"She was reaching around for him even as another couple was offering her their condolences. When Cole stood in front of her, she grasped both his arms the way you once did and said, "He loved you like a son. And then she repeated it."

"I did love Cole like a son. What did he do?"

"He broke and left abruptly and when he was in the safety of his car he wept bitterly. You believed in him. You gave him hope."

"He was my friend."

"And he treasured that more than you know."

I started to inquire about being summoned to the throne, but Paul merely shook his head. I made the wise decision to be silent as we walked together quietly. A man was walking toward us, strumming a guitar, and singing, "Old Rugged Cross." The sight of his black clothes made me laugh. "I guess Johnny Cash is still the man in black."

"His heart is pure light," Paul answered.

I nodded and decided it might be best for this particular minister to refrain from observations for the remainder of this journey.

As we drew near there were angels all around the throne and they sang continuously. He is worthy. He is worthy. There is so much light emanating from the throne that if I had human eyes—it would blind me as it did Paul on the road to Damascus.

Jesus walked down the steps to me. He embraced me. "Cole will be arriving soon."

I nodded my head and thought of the wife he would leave behind. It was my same concern when my time came.

"That is my concern as well, David."

"Should I tell anyone?"

"No."

"What about Petra? She has waited so long on that hill. And Sydny has been there with her a long time as well."

He laughed heartily. "And spoil my surprise."

"I understand." I paused for several moments. "Will his wife be okay?"

"She is a woman of great faith." Moments passed before he added, "She is also a woman who has great love and devotion for her husband."

"I know that you will help her. She will still be heartbroken. I understand that she is much younger than Cole. Perhaps in time."

"She has only truly loved but one man. He was my vessel for her as she was for him."

I waited patiently for him to explain. I knew that there was more to their story.

"She never saw herself as beautiful. He never saw her as anything but."

"Is he sick?"

"Yes."

"But you won't heal him?"

"No," he replied gently. "He also has to come first and not just because of the age difference."

"Why?"

"I don't want him heartbroken again. He might sink back into that dark hole of depression."

"And she won't?"

"She has always proven to be the one of stronger faith, and that is not to discount Cole's belief. He has come a long way, and he has gained much wisdom. Much of that he learned from you and much he acquired after he turned to me with all of his heart.

"There is much I love about Cole. I love his simplicity and his unwillingness to engage in anything bordering on being judgmental. He is not a teacher of my word as you were, but he makes things simple for those around him to understand. When people discuss what is morally right and what is not. He will not tie the debate to rules. He merely states that he has discovered that the more of my spirit he allows inside his heart—the more the other stuff floated away. He needs no laws of the church because my spirit inside of him serves the purpose of right and wrong."

"Does he know that Petra and Sydny are here?"

"No."

He smiled and embraced me. I thanked him, and I walked down the steps with Paul. Peter approached us and said, "I will walk with you, David."

Paul walked in the other direction and it was just the two of us. "Did you know that you are Cole's favorite biblical person?"

"I did not," he replied. "Why do you think that is?"

I chuckled softly. "Because you always were a man of great heart. Your emotions got you into trouble at times just as his have done in his life. He relates to that. He also never viewed the denial as the main part of your story but rather chose to see all that you accomplished for the kingdom after that."

He nodded his head gently. "I look forward to talking with him."

"He will as well my friend." I informed him that I was going to visit Petra and Sydny. He nodded and walked away.

Hopefully, Sydny will remember not to ask unwanted questions because I have just been told I can't share the news of Cole's arrival and no one lies here.

14 ~ Cole

I walked through the main building and emerged on the other side. I could see open land for several hundred feet—ending at a border of tall pine trees. The borders of each side of the open land are woods, composed primarily of pine trees, an array of different oaks, sweetgum, and red maples. There are seventy-seven acres of land in total.

The three main buildings formed a U-shape. I checked the buildings on each side but while they contained plenty of animals and some volunteers—there was no sign of my wife.

I walked back outside and looked in the open field. Movement to my left drew my attention and a horse with a rider emerged and galloped toward me. Mac, the horse she is riding, is a chestnut-colored Morgan. The horse was a rescue—discovered by a photographer while she was taking landscape pictures in a rural area of West Virginia. She heard a noise from a barn that was so tattered that it appeared on the brink of collapse. There she discovered Mac—malnourished and severely underweight.

She made some phone calls and someone placed her in contact with my wife. I drove Ava to rescue this damaged horse. We loaded Mac in the trailer, and brought him here, but not before Ava shared a few choice words with the owner of the horse who could not understand what all the fuss was about and demanded to be compensated. The deputy that accompanied us gave him a choice. Sign the papers relinquishing Mac or be arrested for cruelty to animals. He quickly signed the papers. Mac has been here for over five years and is so beautifully sleek that you would never surmise that he was once so skinny you could count his every rib.

Her smile broadened as she advanced. How do I deliver the news of my impending demise? She is just shy of sixty years old. I drink in the sight of her riding toward me—her long dark, curly hair flowing in the wind. She wore a wheat-colored cowboy hat, or in this case, is it called a cowgirl hat? She wore jeans, a black and white plaid flannel shirt, and pale blue cowboy boots. We have never bought stuff just to have it. No fancy cars or living in a house with far more room than we would ever need. Showing off is not something that is in either of us and if it were I would not blame God if he took from us all that he had so easily given.

That is not to say that we are so high and mighty that we did not splurge occasionally. She loves boots. I mean the girl can't wait for fall to arrive so that she can break them out. She owns about two dozen pairs, and there would be more but she made me promise not to buy any more. I like spoiling her, and she appreciates every little gesture or gift that I have ever given her.

My mind drifted back to our wedding day and in particular the song we slow danced to. The song was "Storm," by Lifehouse. It was our wedding song but my song to her—a song I was not familiar with at the time is "Bless the Broken Road" by Rascal Flatts.

I had been in love before she entered my life. I did not love often but when I did—I held little in reserve. When some of those relationships ended—I was emotionally exhausted and the borderline depression that had plagued me for much of my life became a roaring pit of darkness.

I prayed for God to save those broken roads, but they were shattered for a reason. I should have never embarked down them. I had no idea that he had something and in particular someone better for me. He was just waiting for me to come to him. I am not sure what being a Christian is for people. I think that we all realize it is more than attending church and having your name on a membership roll or at least I hope we all do. The thought I could never shake while I pursued the things that I thought I needed to be happy is that God was waiting for me to turn it all over to him and to simply follow where he said go.

She dismounted and kissed Mac on the side of his face. He snorted happily and raised his head and nodded it twice.

She hugged me and when I did not hug her hard enough to suit her—she said what she often said to me. "Boy, hug me like you mean it."

I hugged her strongly. "A hug like that would crush a petite woman," I said dryly. It was an oft-repeated joke that she did not laugh at initially as she does now. She discovered long ago that I once preferred to date petite fitness women. That was before I had the good sense to give my heart to her.

"You don't need any petite woman when you got me," she replied as she kissed me.

She is just under five feet seven inches and her weight fluctuates from one fifty to one seventy. She worried about my past initially and whether she could measure up to the women I had dated. It was they that could never hold a candle to her.

She had her trust in a man violated once before. We all have our share of scars. I think she always trusted me, but she had seen women operate and manipulate so she worried I might be caught in a compromising position. I knew better even when my first novel was published by a small press and a girl made a move on me right in front of Ava. I confess to not handling it well. The truth is I was shocked. Don't get me wrong. I did nothing to encourage the girl. I just did not react quickly and think to take my wife's hand or place my arm around her. A small gesture that would convey as I have often said to Ava. "I know where my bread gets buttered."

She has become so trusting over the years—she has kissed me goodbye as I occasionally went out on the road alone to do book signings, though she is usually right there at the table with me. I want her there. Having a career as a writer is so fulfilling but having her to share it with me makes it complete.

She looked at me sternly but with a mischievous twinkle in her eyes. "You know I will never be one of those petite women you previously dated."

I smiled. "You have always been perfect for me. In every way." My voice caught a bit and I had hoped that she did not notice. I should have known better.

"What is wrong, baby?" she asked as she gently rubbed the side of my head. It is one of the most endearing gestures that she does for me.

I held her face delicately and said, "Ava, I need you to listen to me." Touching her face is another of the funny little things we share.

During our first year together anytime I touched her face she would audibly gasp and forget where she was at or what she was saying. She talks a lot more than me and one day she discovered that I had begun to employ this little tactic to quieten her. After she ascertained that—she just kept right on jabbering. I would shake my head gently and remind her of when she would go still at my touch.

"That was before you began to use it as a ploy to shush me," she would state firmly, pretending to be mad, but she was not. As the years rolled by, we were hardly ever cross with each other. The day we got married we had a few scriptures read by friends. Ephesians 4:26, *In your anger do not sin": Do not let the sun go down while you are still angry.* We did our best that whatever disagreements we may have and like all married couples we sure had them—that we tabled them and did not go to sleep irritated with each other. It was a vow not only to each other but to God. We honored it pretty well for the most part.

I hate sharing my news, but I have delayed as long as possible. Tears are already falling gently down her cheeks and before I can say it, she pulled me in tight and said, "The cancer is back."

I heard a whine and felt a bump against my knee. I know that it is Daisy. She is a black lab that has been with us for as long as Mac. I was driving the truck home with the horse trailer containing Mac in a rainstorm the night we rescued him. Ava thought that she saw a reflection of eyes in the headlights along an isolated area in the mountains of southern Virginia. I saw nothing. She insisted that I stop and as it is in most things I complied. The road was winding, and it took several hundred feet for me to find a safe place to park on the shoulder of the road. I put my hazard flashers on, and we walked back along the road for several minutes.

Daisy was lying on the side of the road. She had no collar and initially we thought she had been hit by a car, but we found no marks. She had missed several meals. What she did possess was the most pleading, kindest eyes that you could imagine.

I jogged back to the truck and grabbed an extra horse blanket. Ava wrapped her in it, and I cradled her gently as we walked back to the truck. We gave her some water that she gulped greedily. My wife always has all sorts of treats and dog food in the truck. We put a little food in a bowl and she consumed it in seconds. She wanted more but Ava petted her soothingly and whispered that was all for now until she could see how she handled her first food in perhaps days.

"She is full-blooded and around here there is a chance that she is someone's hunting dog. I don't know how we could find the owner but maybe you can Google the nearest animal shelter."

She looked up at me with a countenance that I had witnessed many times over the year and stated firmly—with no room for debate. "Daisy is coming home with us."

I knew that tone. I also knew to be quiet. Wisdom does indeed come with age.

I did check online for two weeks after we returned home. I was relieved that no one filed a lost dog report describing Daisy.

"Hey, girl," I said kneeling to rub her. Even though we did not take her to our home—she decided long ago that while she loved Ava—I was her person.

Mac snorted and put his nose down on Daisy's back. They are the best of friends, and I guess in some strange way they bonded when they arrived here together that rainy night. Often, we would look for Daisy after she was well enough to roam, and she would be lying right outside of Mac's stable.

Daisy meanders around the property much of the day. She never seems to be in a hurry about anything. I am not certain that I have ever witnessed her really run. Her mellow behavior often reminded me of Pete.

Her first year here—I had to give Ava a heads-up when I arrived. The first several times that Daisy saw me enter the office she became so excited she peed all over everything. After Ava cleaned urine the first dozen times she stated wisely, "How about you call me when you are in the parking lot and Daisy can pee outside." It was a good plan and in time she calmed down enough that she did not christen the floor when I walked into the office. I thought many times about bringing her home but somehow, I felt if she was not part of a home routine that it would not hurt so much when she departed. Now, it appeared pretty certain that I will leave first.

I rose and took Ava's hand. "Let's go sit in the office and talk." She looped the reins on an old-fashioned hitching post made of cedar. As we approached the office, I turned to her. "I'm sorry I did not want dogs in our home after Sydny died. That was wrong."

"You did let me but it just seemed to make you grieve all the more over Sydny. You bought this place and gave me the work I was destined to do."

We sat in opposite chairs. Daisy rested her head on my leg, and I rubbed her gently.

"Chemo again?" Ava asked hesitantly.

I shook my head.

"You won't even try? For me?"

"The doctor said the chemo may give me two more years at the most."

"And without it?"

"Maybe a year."

She shook her head so softly. I was breaking her heart. The last thing I ever desired to do.

"Ava, I feel pretty good right now. I would like to take this time and treasure every second with you. I don't want to spend it crying and complaining about our fate. We have been tremendously blessed."

"I know but it is not enough."

"You can do this."

"But I don't want to," she said with childlike innocence.

She sniffled and then blew her nose that sounded anything like the lady she is. I love that about her as well.

"Wow, I thought you had rescued a duck for a moment."

She smiled through her tears. "I guess you have a plan for this hopefully one year that we have."

"I have to get a few things in order and then I want to load the truck up and drive. I want to see Montana, Yosemite Park, and all the great things that I never took time to see. I want to be in Alaska on my birthday. That has always been my dream place to visit, and I want weeks to see it."

"But will you feel well enough to travel?"

114

"Yes," I answered, without room for debate.

"Before you start speculating—I will be seventy-seven on this birthday. God will grant me the time. Come on sweet girl, you know seventy-seven is a great number. We will be home for Christmas. I know it is hard for you to leave this place for so long, but you have good people that will take care of the animals. And you have Holly."

Holly was a local veterinarian who was our friend and had donated much of her time and effort in providing care for the many animals here.

"This place is important, but nothing outside of God is as important as you, and that one is a close contest—truth be told."

"I know that there are things that I have to set up to provide for Cody and you. Once that is completed, I don't want to spend time talking about cancer once we leave. I want to live and enjoy you."

She nodded and said, "There is one thing that I know already that I will ask you to do."

"Name it."

"I won't want to live in our home without you. That would be too much."

"Okay, what is it that you desire?"

"Let's put the house on the market before we leave and begin the process to build me a small place right here."

"You sure that is what you want?"

"No. What I desire is to go wherever you go."

There was nothing I could say to that.

"I will pick a design. It won't take long. Something functional with no more than two bedrooms and two bathrooms. Maybe your son will visit."

"He will."

She nodded gently. "I know you worry about me out here but remember we have volunteers and the staff we hired. Besides, no one could sneak up on me with all these animals here, and I do know how to use a gun."

"I will have the security system inspected and make upgrades."

She nodded again. The despondency that enveloped her face was

115

hard to bear. "How about we go home and spend some time together," I whispered, with a not-so-subtle wink.

"You feel up to that?"

"I ain't dead yet," I responded with a beaming grin.

"Later, I will grill steaks. We can watch a movie and have popcorn? One of my favorite date nights."

"Do you want to stream a movie or watch something from our movie library?"

"Can we watch Tombstone again?" It is my favorite movie of all time.

"We can do anything you like," she replied.

I looked at Daisy and if I did not know better, I would swear she knew what was going on. I rubbed her head. "Daisy, you are going home with us."

Ava smiled and merely nodded.

"I will call Cody tomorrow and ask him to come home next week. I will not give him news like this over the phone."

"Okay," she agreed. "He will have time. He is out of work."

"Aw, the nature of working in politics. And once again he called the troll and not his dad."

She punched me playfully in the arm. I guess I should explain the whole troll thing. This incredibly funny man, Lou, worked with me many years ago. He did not care for his stepmother. One day at work he said to us, "I am going to Dad's house for dinner tonight. That troll he is married to is probably hiding under the bridge." My coworker, Ralph and I about fell off our chairs in laughter. Lou said it all so dryly—never once joining us in our laughter. He was always like that, and he kept the crew in stitches. I shared this story one night with Ava and Cody shortly after we were married. Upon completion of the story, Ava looked at Cody and stated sternly, "You are never to refer to me as the troll."

The following day Cody returned to his place in Raleigh. It took a few days for us to discover a little something he left behind. Ava had bought a small red lamp for me that resided on my desk. Cody had used the label maker and printed out 'Troll's Lamp.' I flipped the switch to it early one morning and discovered it. I showed it to her and of course, we laughed. It became their joke.

"I think he has finally had his fill of working in the political arena."

"Good, because I have an idea. I will discuss it with him when he arrives."

She gave me a quizzical look and I said, "I will tell you later. Let's go home, baby."

We walked outside hand in hand and somehow Daisy assumed correctly that this time that she was indeed coming home with us.

15 ~ Sydney

Petra and I watched David depart as evening descended upon us. "Petra, David had something on his mind that he didn't want to share."

"You noticed that as well."

"Yes, but I knew not to ask."

"I am very proud of you and the growth you have made. That first day I saw you I could not believe my master loved a little dog like you. He never cared for those yapper dogs."

I sighed heavily. "I know that and you have told that story one time too many." I acted like I was put off but it was just that—an act and Petra knew this.

"I've enjoyed our time on this hill together. I would have understood if you would have chosen to live elsewhere. You had some wonderful families who wanted you to live with them, especially when Ava's grandparents came here." Petra paused for several moments before asking, "Why didn't you? You knew that I would be fine here on this hill. It is not like anyone in Heaven is lonely."

"I wanted to be with you. We will live in a home one day when they come. Regardless of where one of us goes—the other goes as well."

There were a few moments of comfortable silence before I grinned at her and said, "I almost did throw you under the bus to go live with Ben and his family. I mean a little dog like me living with grizzly bears. Now that is a match made in Heaven."

Petra replied with a slight chuckle. "That first day he decided to scoop you up and hold you close you were so scared."

"Well, I use to be a little nervous when Dad first began picking me up. He is over six feet tall as you well know. Ben is over nine feet tall. That would be a long way to fall and before you say anything I know that I would not get hurt if he dropped me, but I didn't know that the first time he held me."

She gazed at the colors and her eyes sparkled. "I love this hill." She paused before adding, "You sure have helped me enjoy this place even more and though I still watch the gate—seeing my master with your mom and how happy they looked, plus all you have shared about her—well, I don't desire for her to be hurt and lonely."

"Petra, I know that God created us to be a companion for people, but I think above all he shaped us to be loyal. He knew that humans would often desert one another and at times only we would be there to comfort them. I did that for Mom, especially before Dad came into the picture. I understand that you did that for Dad as well."

"Your wisdom has grown."

I shrugged a bit like it was no big deal, but I loved hearing her praise. "I did not know what wisdom was until I arrived here. Dad talked about that word a lot. He said that he knew he was not an overly smart man and that was okay because he cared more about gaining wisdom. He did not care for people who were always trying to impress people with their perceived intellect. Intellectuals are the most boring people on the face of the earth I recall him saying."

We stop talking and resumed watching the skies. In the center of it, there was a long trail of the color burgundy running through it. I looked over at Petra, and I am about to ask her if she sees it but I hear her breathing calmly and in such a restful rhythm that I know she is asleep. The longer I am here with her on this hill the more she sleeps. I think that she relaxes more with my company and if she were to sleep through that trumpet signaling the next arrival, she knows that I will wake her if I see our dad. I'm just kidding. No one could sleep through the decibels produced by that trumpet.

I rested my face next to hers and soon I joined her in sleep so peaceful you would have to be with us here on this hill to comprehend it.

16 ~ Cole

Cody arrived from Raleigh and when he walked in the door, he hugged us both warmly and with tears in his eyes he said, "The cancer is back."

As I held him and tears streamed from both of us, I recalled a similar day, when he gave his best man toast at our wedding. There is a picture of us that seizes the moment. I am clutching him and sobbing on his shoulder while he wears a contented smile. Our roles had reversed and he was no longer a little boy holding his dad but rather it was his dad clinging to the young man that he had become.

He always did have the most tender of hearts. That is one of his many gifts and the one I am most proud of.

Cody worked at the local movie theater in Carolina Beach, through high school, and during college breaks. It closed down soon after he graduated from college. Occasionally, I joked as we passed by the empty building that if I ever had a book takeoff that I was buying that place and restoring it. I knew it would never be a big moneymaker and breaking even would be a small miracle. Oh, the summers would do well enough with the tourists, but the off-season would prove very slow.

One day when I deposited a rather substantial check for my third book, I decided that it was time to make a silly dream a reality. We bought the property and renovated the small four-room viewing complex. We also upped the menu just a bit. Nothing fancy and you could surely purchase the typical movie fare of popcorn, snacks, and soft drinks, but Ava decided that offering quesadillas would be simple and easy. They proved to be a hit. We also added a few beer and wine selections.

The movie theater began to show a profit in the fourth year. I mean this in no way to brag about my good deeds. I did not need the money from the business. If there was a decent profit at the end of the year, we put it back into the business and gave the employees a bonus. We took no profits. We also admitted church groups free of charge at special viewing times when a Christian film was released.

Ava, Cody, and I were spending a day on the beach the day after he came home. I had an idea for my unemployed son. He could come home and manage the movie theater. My manager had recently turned in his resignation.

I made him an offer that he could not refuse. I would hire him at a very good salary for the next five years to manage the theater, at which point he could do with it as he so chose. Sell it. Keep running it. I encouraged but did not demand that he try to keep it as a movie house for the residents of Pleasure Island.

He accepted my offer and then he asked Ava a question that warmed me to the point where I thought my heart might burst. He said he would like to live with her for a while after I was gone. She readily agreed as they hugged each other fiercely and shed their tears on each other. I watched in amazement at the goodness of our God, but he was not done yet.

It was later in the day when I drove the four of us to the Carolina Beach State Park to watch the sunset bed down over the river. Yes, I said four. For the first time since I drove Sydny to this same spot, a dog was going along for the ride. Daisy sure enjoyed her first trip through the park. She stared the deer down on the shoulder of the road just as Sydny had done so many years ago.

We watched the last sparks of color dance over the river when my son turned from the front passenger seat and looked at me with a sad smile. "Dad, I have held on to my dreams and the things that I thought defined me. On the drive here I stole your line. God, you take the wheel. I want you to have all of me and not just the parts that I want to give."

I merely nodded at the sincerity and the light in his eyes. From the back, I heard the sound of tears. Daisy decided it was a good time for her to climb up front despite my protests and perched her sixty pounds in Cody's lap. She moaned softly and licked his face.

We all laughed heartily.

Ava and I spent the next several weeks preparing for our last trip together and for my departure. I always wanted to go first. I guess that is pretty selfish of me. She remained strong and firm when we are together, but sometimes, I heard weeping coming from another room, and I rethink what I desire and think it is better that she goes first and I remained alone, though I don't think I would last one week without her. I fear my old nemesis depression might visit me for the first time in many years, and this time I might not be strong enough to survive the battle. All I know to do right now is to try to live out the old song, "Walk by Faith," by Jeremy Camp—the best that I can.

God has been with us. Even in the face of death, he has chosen to be ever so gracious. We put our house on the market and it sold in two days. The owners paid us with one certified check. We negotiated for them to take over thirty days from the closing date. We placed that money in an account for Ava. The builders have already begun construction, and they promised that all of it will be completed by the time we returned from our lengthy trip. I am asking God for a birthday with my wife in Alaska and to be home for one last Christmas.

I have no clue why but suddenly I recall a prayer that I asked God for long ago. It was shortly after Sydny died, and I wanted to know if indeed we would see him again and if that were true—then that meant that I would see Pete again as well. I never shared this with anyone—not even Ava. I sat on the beach one day mourning the huge loss this little guy left behind when I asked God for that sign. There were two porpoises in front of us that day, and I asked at some point to see seven in a circle. I never received that vision—not while looking at the ocean or even in a dream. All these years later, I still cling to the hope that *The Rainbow Bridge* is real, but I waver in my belief if it is true.

17 ~ Cole

It was November first and as I predicted I have made it to age seventy-seven. We have seen so many wonderful sights on this trip that I do not realize that God is about to show one that trumps all.

We have driven through many states, but we saved most of our time for the areas out West that neither of us had seen. I pointed the truck in the directions of the Dakotas and Wyoming where we spent a fair amount of time. After that it was Montana and I could have spent months exploring that expansive, beautiful state.

We have seen the streams where *A River Runs Through It* was filmed. There were mountains so majestic and powerful that we stood in awe—speechless. We explored Yosemite Park, as well as almost one week in the Grand Canyon area. I have had the energy to hike believe it or not. I don't mean that I have scaled a five-thousand-foot mountain but if the trail proved smooth enough and I paced myself—God has granted me the strength to press on.

We marveled at Idaho, Oregon, and the state of Washington. We were in Alaska by early October. We planned to see all that we could of this wondrous state and then begin the long drive home on the second day of November.

It was after three in the afternoon, and we were in Nome, Alaska, looking out at the Bering Sea. We had charted a flight from Anchorage where we were staying. We discovered a house in Anchorage that was cheaper to rent monthly, even if we did not stay the entire time. It was our base from which we chartered flights, or took nice drives, or spent nights in another town.

God granted us favor and opened the best doors for the trip. I knew that I had little time left on this earth, and I do hate leaving my wife whom I adore, however, I don't think I can ask more of God than he has delivered.

We sat on rocks and gazed out at the sea together. The sky was faultless, and I have no clue how far we can see at this moment. Ava's head is nestled on my shoulder, and I leaned mine into her. Our faces touched. I thought I knew love before her, but she has truly taught me what love is. She is 1 Corinthians 13.

Daisy's head is in my lap. I have a firm grasp of her collar to make sure she does not slide down. Sadly, I am too old to retrieve her if she were to fall down the rocks into the ocean. Truthfully, though there was little to worry about. She reminded me of Pete. She was content just to be near me. I know Pete wandered off the night she met her demise, but I was not home. She like Daisy never desired to leave my side.

The pilot, Herman, had been inspecting the plane, though I suspected he was just finding things to do to grant us time alone. He is a good and cautious pilot, and we have hired him several times to fly us to a destination that we wanted to visit.

I heard him approach. I think that all of us had our eyes closed. Now I know you wonder how could I know if Ava and Daisy's eyes are closed if mine are, and I am not peeping like we did as small children when we were supposed to close our eyes at the dinner table while Mom said grace, but both are them are snoring slightly, and I may be venturing out on a limb here, but I don't think either of them is snoring with their eyes open.

Suddenly Daisy stood and barked, stirring all of us. I gripped her collar tighter. I looked at the sea, and I began to laugh heartily. Ava stood and pointed to the sea. "Wow! Look."

"I have never seen anything quite like that," Herman said in a surprised voice.

I guess by now that you would like to know what the amazing sight is. There were seven porpoises swimming continuously in a tight circle. They did this for five minutes at least before a couple of them did a couple of flips to show off and then they departed.

"Those were Dall's porpoises. I could tell by their black backs, white bellies, and their size."

Ava eyed me quizzically.

"When I was reading about things pertaining to Alaska, I recall

126

reading about them."

"We need to be going," Herman said. "Not a whole lot of day-light remaining for this time of year and I would prefer to fly while it is still light."

I never stopped smiling as we walked to the plane. Sydney and Pete were indeed in Heaven—even Amanda, my crazy beagle was prob-ably roaming freely there with no danger of cars. I would see them soon.

That night as we settled in for our last evening in Anchorage, I shared with Ava what the porpoises meant.

She merely nodded and said, "Please tell my little boy I hope to see him soon."

The next morning, I woke in great pain and fatigue like I have never known. I still believed God would allow me to endure through Christmas, but the unbelievable energy that I had enjoyed on this trip had dissipated. I knew it would not return.

Ava wanted to take me to the hospital but I refused. "We are going home. Call the airport and check on flights."

"What about your truck?"

"I will take care of that. Please give me my phone."

I took the phone and called Herman while Ava called for flights.

"Hello, Cole. I thought that you would be on the road by now."

"Little bit of a problem. I need some help. Are you busy this morning?"

"I have no trips chartered today. Days are getting shorter and business is slowing."

"I noticed your truck has seen better days."

He laughed and replied, "You want to give me that nice four-wheel-drive Toyota Tundra that you are driving?"

"Yes. As a matter of fact, I do."

There was silence on the other end.

"Herman, I am worn out. I can't drive back home."

Ava mouthed to me that there were no available flights until to-morrow. I nodded to her.

"We were going to fly home, though Ava just said there are no seats available on any flights that will get us going in that direction today."

"I will help you out with that, but you don't need to give me your truck. Pay someone to drive it."

"No."

Silence again. I guess it is not often that someone offers to give you a truck that is less than two years old.

"I do need a favor when we can find a flight."

"Name it."

"Help my wife get our stuff together and drive us to the airport. Draw up a simple paper that says I am giving you the truck, and we will get it notarized. When we get home, I will mail you the title."

"I don't know what to say."

"Say yes. Consider it a tip. You have shown us things that I have dreamed about much of my adult life. Alaska was always my dream vacation. I never was much for traveling."

"Let me call you right back."

I agreed and put the phone away.

Five minutes later my phone vibrated. It was Herman.

"I got you a direct flight to Raleigh. From there you are on your own."

Now it was my turn to be silent.

"My brother is the manager at the airport. He worked it out and for Daisy as well."

"Thank you. You can drive us to the airport in your new truck."

"You don't have to."

"I know. One more favor I ask of you."

"Name it."

"Don't make a big deal out of it."

"Okay," he replied and then he paused as he searched for his next words. "I have a favor to ask."

"Name it."

"The way you laughed about the porpoises led me to believe there is something more to the story."

"I will share that with you on the way to the airport."

"You rest. I will be right over and help Miss Ava get your things together."

"Thank you." I placed the phone down again and asked Ava to call Cody and ask him to pick us up and drive us home.

I fell asleep on the couch and did not wake until they roused me to get in the truck. Herman and Ava had loaded all our bags while I slept. I told Herman the story of Sydney and the porpoises on the way.

Herman parked the truck in a no parking zone right by the front entrance. A very well-dressed executive type opened my door for me. He was tall and lean, much like his brother. He had a perfectly kept close cut beard that was black with specks of gray.

"You have to be Herman's brother."

"And very proud to be so," he stated as he looked over at his brother and nodded. "My name is Randy, and we are going to make this as easy for you as possible."

Three people stood behind him waiting for direction. Turning to them, he said, "Please gather their bags and assist them with anything they need."

He looked to the back and began to pet Daisy. "I know that you don't want to be away from your family." He turned to the lone female member of the staff. "Ashley, I know you have a brother nearby that has a service dog. Do you think we can borrow a vest for Daisy? Tell him to purchase another one and send me the bill."

"I will call him right now, sir," she replied. "He always has a spare vest." She walked away briskly as she made the call. Seconds later, she turned and called to Randy. She made a thumbs up gesture.

I noticed one of the airport guards approaching. I always love it when people are walking toward you, but they can't wait until they get close enough to speak in a normal tone of voice but somehow feel the need to assert their authority by commanding you in a loud tone from several yards away. "Let's move that truck right this second, or I will have it towed."

Randy was helping Ava out of the back seat and when he had completed that task he turned to the approaching guard. "Back off," he said firmly without raising his voice.

The guard blinked when he realized that he had just shouted orders to a group that included his boss. "Sorry, Mr. Dickens," he said

129

sheepishly and abruptly turned and walked hurriedly back in the direction that he came from.

Randy shrugged and offered, "He probably needs to drink decaf."

Everything was loaded and we were about to be escorted past all the security checks straight to our plane.

"Do you need a wheelchair?" Randy asked gently, not wanting to bruise my male ego.

I was exhausted, but there was no way I was being rolled anywhere. "Thank you, but no. I will lean on Ava."

She had her arm around me and nodded in agreement. I turned to her and whispered in her ear. "A petite woman would fall right over."

She smacked me very lightly on my arm as she smiled through the tears that she unsuccessfully tried to blink back.

It was time to say goodbye to Herman. Ava hugged him warmly. Backing away he tipped his faded blue cap and said, "God bless you, ma'am." She kissed him on the cheek and he blushed. My wife had melted another male heart just as she had mine many years prior.

I shook his hand. He looked at me and said firmly, "It is not often in a man's life when you meet someone and you know that you will never be the same for that encounter. I guess you would answer that it is not you but rather who resides in you."

I nodded.

"Life is tough here but I love it. Business is hit or miss. The gift of that truck is a big deal."

I nodded again—too weary for words.

"Randy has offered me a job here for far more money, but I just love flying. Even more, I love flying people like Miss Ava and you to places that existed previously only in your imagination. The wonder that appears in your eyes. Well, it is hard to put a price tag on something like that."

"You should do what you enjoy big brother," Randy interjected.

Herman hugged Ava again and whispered something in her ear. She nodded in agreement and kissed him once again on the cheek. She delicately wiped away the lipstick that was left behind.

***

It was Christmas night. I have made it this far, but I know that there is little time left. I look forward to escaping this ever-increasing pain, but the wound in Ava's eyes pushes me to hang on just a little while longer.

Cody is with us, and we have had a grand Christmas. We chose not to do gifts this year and to just enjoy each other's company. I don't know if they celebrate Christmas in Heaven or perhaps every day is Christmas. I am going to leave here without many if not most of the answers. That is okay. I have learned to fill in the blanks with faith.

We were sitting on the long front porch of the newly construct-ed house on the ranch in new steel gray Adirondack chairs. I worried that my staying here would bring too many memories for Ava once I am gone. She said that she would be all right. It was not like the beach house where everything was a memory of our beginning. I hope that proves so.

I started to rise, and Ava stood quickly to assist me. "I am just going to the bathroom. I will be right back." I took a step toward the door, and Daisy was right by my side. Ever since the morning in Alaska when I woke, knowing that my fuel gauge was on empty—never to be filled again. Daisy has refused to allow me out of her sight. Dogs, how is it that they know so much?

I don't like Ava hovering over me. I have insisted that she go about her chores while I sit here on this new porch, not waiting to die as much as waiting to live forever. I have not seen Mom and Grandma in so very long. I believe I will see them soon. I will enjoy leisurely walks with David. I will see Jesus—face to face.

I opened the door, and Daisy waited for me to step into the room and once I did, she followed. I bent down—pushing back the pain to rub her head. "You are a good girl. I am counting on you to watch over those two when I am gone."

She whined softly. "Now that I know I will see Pete and Sydny again—I am certain that you will be with us one day as well. You are so much like Pete that it can't be a coincidence. God, my Father, loving me to the tiniest details of my life."

131

I fell last week when a surge of pain caused me to black out temporarily. I have refused morphine and chose milder sedatives to combat the pain. I want my remaining days to be clear. Ava was outside with the animals while I remained on the floor unable to rise.

I woke to the sound of Daisy's furious barking. She kept running to the door and back to me. Ava must not have closed the door properly when she left. That is the only explanation I have, as to how Daisy was able to open the door and run for help.

She found Ava riding Mac through a trail in the woods. She barked furiously at her and then turned to run back toward me. Ava gave Mac a good nudge, and he galloped through the remainder of the trail and then in the open pastures—delivering her right at the front porch. Ava helped me up and assisted me to the couch. She started to call 911 when I said firmly, "No. There is nothing they can really do for me, and I am not going to the hospital or Hospice. I'm okay. You can look me over but nothing is broken. I might have a bruise. I just got light headed and fell." I smiled at her and said, "I'm not quite as strong as I once was." I chuckled and added, "I always wanted my weight to be below two hundred pounds—but not this way. Most of the muscle from years of exercise is gone." My weight hovered around two hundred-twenty-five for most of my years with Ava. I was down fifty pounds from that.

She examined me carefully and concurred with my diagnosis. Daisy waited for her to move and then she carefully jumped on the couch and nestled next to me—her head resting on my chest. Ava stroked her back with long rubs and told her what a good girl she was.

I returned from my trip to the bathroom and eased back into my chair. Daisy, seeing me safely in it rested at my feet. Ava covered me with a blanket and kissed me gently on my lips. She then held my face and said, "Thank you. I dreamed and prayed for you and when you came you were more than I expected. You always have made me feel so loved—so beautiful."

I heard Cody sniffle and fight back tears. Reaching up I touched her face and said, "You are loved and you always were beautiful. God just sent me to help you realize it."

She returned to her chair, and the three of us sat quietly for several minutes. "Dad, can we talk just a little bit of business?"

"Sure. What do you have?"

"I've been crunching the numbers, and it seems it would be wise to close the theater for January and February and that time can be used for maintenance and any renovations that are warranted."

"What about the staff? Those high school and college kids can't go two months without a paycheck. We also have those two widow ladies on staff. They rely on that income to supplement their social security."

"When I ran the numbers, my idea was that each year they worked from March to the end of the year—there would be a two-month paid vacation for them based on how many hours they worked. The numbers still work. It is cost effective to not only close down but we can pay them their salary and still come out with a profit. It also should prove to keep staff turnover down."

I turned to my son. "That sounds good."

He smiled and said, "Who knows? The way the Island is growing—winters might not prove so slow in the future but for now, I think this is the right way to go."

"It's your business to run."

We heard a car approach and park in the driveway in front of the house.

"I wonder what Holly is doing here? Ava asked.

"How do you know it is Holly?" Cody asked.

"Who else would it be?" Ava asked.

Holly is our veterinarian friend. She had done quite well with her practice in Wilmington, and she was always available to assist Ava with any problems with the animals, especially the horses. That was her love, and I enjoyed watching the two of them ride away and spend time together doing something that they both loved.

I heard the car door close. "Go get her, Daisy."

Daisy looked anxiously at me, and I knew she did not want to leave me even for a moment.

"Go," I commanded in as firm a voice as I could muster.

Moments later Holly and Daisy approached. Daisy immediately returned and laid down at my feet.

"Mind if I pull up a chair?"

Cody pulled a rocker away from the wall and placed it in the row with us. She sat and rocked gently.

Holly is in her early forties. She is dressed in blue jeans and a flannel plaid shirt with a deep brown LL Bean barn coat over it. Her brown hair is pulled back in a ponytail. She has slight freckles on a baby face that I don't think will ever age. But my favorite part of Holly is that she has a warm smile with a mischievous twinkle that is often present in her deep brown eyes.

"What are you doing out here on Christmas night, and where is Thad?" Ava asked.

"He is fine. I am certain that he is asleep in his recliner by now. I told him to go to bed, but he insisted on waiting up for me. I told him that I wanted to check on the animals."

"The animals are fine."

"I know."

We sat for several minutes in silence before I broke the stillness of the Christmas night. "What do you have on your mind?"

She breathed in heavily before sharing what was on her heart. "I love coming here and caring for the animals. Don't get me wrong. I love my practice, but this is different." She was silent again for several moments.

Ava reached over and grabbed her hand. "I could have never done this without you and all the help you gave so generously."

She shook her head. "No, it is you that gave me a chance to give back, and now if you guys agree I would like to try and give a little more?"

"What do you mean?" Ava asked.

"Thad and I have done pretty well for ourselves. He is the Vice President of GE, and my practice has been blessed. I would like to sell it to the two vets that have been with me for the past fifteen years and help out here full time."

"You are doing this to watch after me when Cole is…" Ava's voice trailed off.

"Partly, but also because I can do this. God has blessed us greatly, and Thad is fine with my decision."

"But…" I uttered before being interrupted by Holly.

"It's a done deal. We are looking at buying property and building a home nearby and selling our home in Wilmington. I already talked to the doctors that I work with and they are financially able and ready to buy me out. Everything falling into place. God's hand," she whispered as she gazed at the stars.

Ava turned to me and asked, "This place is really mine?"

I chuckled as I recalled getting all my affairs in order courtesy of my attorney, Wylene. I took Ava's hand. "Honey, I don't think I own anything at this point. It is all in your name or Cody's."

"We have him right where we want him, Troll," Cody said as he winked at her.

She turned back to Holly. "Build your house here. There is plenty of land. I talked with Cody about this and we are facing changes that I don't like to think about. But when we drew up all the papers on this place, which I now own, I stated in my will that it was to go to you when my time comes. I have no children of my own except for my stepson, and he calls me the troll so I am not giving it to him. Plus, the only thing he knows about animals is how to pet them. Like his dad here, he is too afraid to ride a horse or even get near them. Talk with Thad and we will ride out tomorrow and you guys can pick a home site."

"I didn't see any of this coming," Holly said. "If it ever is my property, I want you to know that I won't sell this place, and I will keep it going the way I think that you would want."

"I know," Ava answered, before adding, "But don't be afraid to put your stamp on the place."

Holly turned to Cody. "Are you sure that this is okay with you? Please say so if it is not."

Cody laughed softly. "What would I do with this place? Like Mom said, the only thing I know how to do with animals is pet them, and that is pretty much limited to dogs."

He looked at me, before turning back to Holly. "Dad has been more than generous to me. I don't need this land or quite frankly the headaches of managing it, and I could never sell it and displace these animals."

She nodded and then her eyes grew wide. "Oh my gosh! I forgot." She took off in a hurry to her SUV.

She returned moments later with a tiny, shy, brown Chihuahua. "Ava told me that you lost your little dog earlier this year, and this one needs a home. He was dropped off at our front door in a cardboard box earlier this week. I have checked him out really well. He is in good shape. He wasn't malnourished. No worms or other health issues. He appears to be about ten months old."

She placed the little guy in Cody's arms, and he immediately snuggled in close to Cody's chest and relaxed. The little guy seemed to know he was home.

Looking around at everyone my heart was so warm. Ava sensed this and turned to me. She began to cry. "I don't know that I can honestly say I will be okay without you. I can't imagine not waking each morning to you holding me in your arms. And I want to thank you for not giving me that speech that I am young enough to love again. I have no interest in filling time with another when I have had the love of my life with you, Cole Banks."

"Have I been a good husband?" It was a question I had asked often in our marriage but I would word it, "Am I a good husband?" Each time she would offer a look of slight bewilderment that I would ask such a question. But each time she would one up my question and offer, "Are you kidding? You are a great husband."

This time she said softly as she touched my face. "Beyond compare."

There was silence as my wife held my hand. We have held hands a million times. What is it about holding hands that in some ways seems more intimate than a kiss? I profess that I do not have the answer.

She gripped my hand tighter. "I know that you are hurting, and I don't want you to fight it for me. Go home. I will be there soon, or I sure hope I am. I have begged God to allow me to go with you, but it appears that he has other plans."

There were tears everywhere. I stood and the four of us wrapped our arms around each other and cried for several minutes. I could feel Daisy pressed into the back of my legs. We said our goodnights. Holly

136

drove away, and the rest of us went inside.

Ava helped me to bed and tucked me in. She kissed me softly on the lips.

"I might wake you up a little later," I said as I winked.

"That has never been a problem," she answered. "Get some rest. I will be back shortly."

She went outside, and I heard her talking to someone on the phone, but I fell deeply asleep, unable to decipher her words.

18 ~ Cole

It was mid-afternoon. The last day of the year. The weather is so warm that I am wearing shorts and a long sleeve black tee shirt. I sat on the porch and watched Ava ride Mac across the field. "Lord, how did I wind up with such a beautiful woman in every way? I once believed that you were not really for me as much as I hoped but when you thought I was good enough for her that changed everything."

Ava rode up to the porch and dismounted. She was reading a text on her phone as she walked toward me. She kissed me and then she kissed Daisy right on top of the head. "Good girl. Always looking after my husband."

We both turned upon hearing a car door close. "Company?" I asked. "I hope no one wants to celebrate because I am not up for a New Year's Eve party."

"A surprise," she said as she walked away.

Moments later she returned with a woman that I did not know. She wore a long gray dress. Her hair was blonde and she wore it in a ponytail. She wore stylish, slightly large, deep blue glasses with ear rings that matched. "This is Becky," she said.

I was confused until Becky said, "I believe you know my husband."

I turned my head slightly—not understanding and that is when Herman walked around the corner. "Do you need a pilot?" he asked with a sheepish smile.

"Where I am going, I think that is covered but thanks for the offer."

The smiles turned inward quickly.

"Hey, none of that. We have to have a little humor around here. What are you doing here?"

"Ava has called me a few times to tell me how you were doing.

The last time was Christmas night. I mentioned it to Randy. His response was, 'Brother you know I can fly you free anywhere you want to go—so here we are."

"That is very kind of you, but you did not need to go to all this trouble."

"Yes, he did," his wife replied firmly—leaving no room for debate.

Ava pulled up chairs and we sat and talked for two hours. The sun hung low in the cobalt sky. They stood to leave and said they would return tomorrow. We said our goodbyes, and the couple from Alaska walked toward their vehicle. Moments later, Becky returned alone. She stood below us on the ground directly in front of me.

"Something on your mind?" I inquired.

She nodded and smiled warmly. "Herman is a good man. Not perfect by any means but still a good honest man. He has always done right by me. Sure, he has drunk more at times than I would prefer and occasionally when he is frustrated his language can turn salty. I always believed and attended church, but he refused to go with me."

She paused and I waited for her to continue. "It was after midnight that day he drove Ava and you to the airport and came home with a truck we sorely needed. I could not believe our good fortune. The truck, however, was only the beginning.

"We had gone to bed about nine as usual, and I woke and he wasn't there. That is not that uncommon. He did a tour in Afghanistan long ago. I think what he witnessed there keeps him up some nights, though he has always refused to talk about it. Many times, I have found him nursing a couple of drinks of Jim Beam—trying to quiet the noise in his head.

"This night was different. I walked into the kitchen. There was a new bottle of Jim Beam with an empty glass beside it resting on the table. He was sitting there, reading the Bible and when he saw me—he looked more peaceful than I can ever recall.

"He smiled and said softly, 'I didn't drink anything.' Now, he is not an alcoholic, and I would not want you to think that. He takes flying too seriously. But on sleepless nights he sought solace in a couple of drinks and nothing so bad about that but on this night—he sought comfort in the Bible.

"He told me that he would like to start attending church with me and that he wanted to be baptized."

She was crying now, and my wife who cried so easily joined her. I blinked back my tears.

"God did it, but you were the vessel he used." She bent down and hugged me fiercely. It hurt me a bit, but I was not about to tell her. She let go of me and kissed me on top of my head. "God bless you Cole Banks, and you as well Miss Ava." She walked away briskly.

***

I was sitting in my chair on the porch. New Year's Day arrived with plentiful sunrise. The ground was damp and a few puddles displayed the rain that arrived sometime during the wee hours of the morning when we were asleep. I think it thundered at some point, but I can't be certain if that was real or part of a dream. Thunder led me to think of Sydny, and I bet he was not afraid of it any longer—if indeed it ever thundered in Heaven. I am certain that I am about to learn so many fresh things.

Ava walked to my side and took my worn, black and chrome coffee mug. "I will get you another cup of coffee," she said, leaning in to kiss me.

She took a step and then turned back to me. "You wear those sunglasses a lot lately," she stated as she pointed to my face. "Even when the light is faint," she added.

"My eyes are weary, and they always were sensitive to light but much more so now."

She nodded and kissed me once again and then she held my face with one hand and said, "Love you, baby boy and those beautiful blue eyes."

"Love you, sweetheart."

"I will be back in just a minute with your coffee."

But I had departed for my true home by the time she returned.

141

19 ~ Sydny

It was the end of another evening on the hill. I was in my cutest position—paws stretched out forward with my adorable head buried in the center. The trumpet sounded, and I casually lifted my head to observe those entering the gate.

Petra watched far more intently than I did. She was sitting up, and I pawed at her chest. She looked down kindly at me. "He will be here one day. I know you have waited a lot longer than me."

She gazed down at the village and she saw David walking with Cole's mom. David must have sensed us looking because he turned suddenly and waved. He had a broad smile imprinted upon his face.

Was it any wonder why Dad loved this dear man so? How could you not? We lost sight of them as they entered the village and blended in with all the others.

Peter began to close the gate, and it was nearly shut. I speculated as I often did about the need for a gate. It is not like anyone is sneaking past God and all his angels to enter his kingdom unaware.

Petra nestled her head briefly on my back. We heard a faint shout from far away. "Hey! Don't close that gate."

We saw a tall man with dark brown hair sprinting for the gate like his life depended on it. I found it peculiar that he was wearing sunglasses. He was dressed in brown cargo shorts and a long sleeve black Carolina Beach tee shirt. "Now what man would enter the gates of Heaven with sunglasses on?" I inquired.

And then Petra took off running for the village in a sprint like you would not believe. I have never witnessed her do more than walk in our time together. Amanda saw her and decided to race her to whatever her destination was. Amanda was fast. She was built for speed and had moves that an NFL running back would covet. Petra blew by her like she was standing still. It appeared to puzzle Amanda so much that she came

143

to an abrupt stop and sat.

Petra raced through the village toward the gate, and I don't know why I am so slow this morning to not ascertain that there was only one event that would provoke her to run like the wind.

"Dad!" I took off as fast as my little Chihuahua legs would take me. Reaching the village, I noticed a congregation waiting at the bottom of the hill. Dad's Mom and Grandma were standing with David. I stopped by their side—unsure of whether I was supposed to wait with them or continue up the hill. Being a little dog, I was having trouble seeing around the people.

I chose to keep working my way to the front of the line. I saw a sight that was well, I would say unbelievable, but we are in Heaven where the unbelievable is believable. Dad was resting on the plush grass and laughing. Petra was on top of him and squirming next to him like she just couldn't get close enough. Oh, what a sight! Sweet Petra had waited so long for her master. I wanted her to have this time but then believe it or not I heard a voice and I knew that it was God.

"Sydny, go welcome your dad."

Well, you don't have to tell me twice. Especially, when the directive comes straight from God. I sprinted up that hill like it was nobody's business.

Dad lifted his head and was still laughing when he saw me. He stood quickly and shouted, "Sydny!"

You may choose not to believe this next part, and that is okay by me, but I know it to be true. I sprinted toward him and somehow, I knew that for this moment I could soar. I was ten feet away when I jumped. I landed right in the center of his chest. He caught me and loved on me something fierce. "Oh, Sydny. How I have missed you."

As we walked toward the crowd that waited his mom and grandma came walking toward them. David waited patiently behind with such a beaming grin on his face. There were others there to greet Dad as he sauntered down the hill—still wearing those sunglasses. It was such a sight to see people loving on him, especially Mom and Grandma. But you know what? He refused to put me down. Oh, what Heaven this was for me—to be held in his arms close to his heart.

And then I heard a voice that was soft but yet so firm at the same time. "*For where your treasure is there lies your heart as well.*"

Dad's eyes grew wide, and he removed those silly sunglasses. I think he just wanted to make an entrance. He sat me down and raced to the feet of the Lord and fell, burying his face in the ground in an unworthy manner, or was it complete respect? I don't know which.

That same soft voice softened. "No child. Rise. You are home." And Jesus and my dad embraced.

20 ~ Petra

I hope you realize by now that there is much that I still don't understand about transitioning to this place. It seems we arrive with memories, and the bad fade while the good ones remain. I am so happy that my master is here—Wait. Make that dad.

One of the first orders of business—so to speak was to ask him if I could call him dad like Sydny does. I was tired of referring to him as my master.

He laughed so freely at my request. I recall now that often his laughter was strained before but not now. He is so happy and he told me, of course, I could refer to him as dad.

As we sat on the hill and watched evening arrive—I enjoyed watching him marvel at the colors. I know that we will not be separated ever again, but I still have not left his side since I ran past everyone to reach him first when he entered the gate. Now that I think about it Sydny has not left him either. Not even when Ben came by and invited Sydny to go for a walk. Dad did get quite a kick out of Sydny's good friend—the mammoth Kodiak Grizzly Bear.

Our first evening sitting on the hill was truly spectacular. The light began to fade slightly and below us was a field of wildflowers as far as you could see. They were deep blue, red, and a few were white. All of a sudden butterflies of every imaginable color began to descend on the flowers. We watched in awe and silence until Dad spoke. "Your mom and I often sat by a flower bed that we had planted. Butterflies were abundant and we enjoyed watching them, but it surely doesn't hold a candle to this. Wow," he added softly.

And then believe it or not it began to get darker than I have ever seen here. Sydny immediately jumped into Dad's lap and quivered slightly. Her protector was with her once again, and it made me feel so warm inside. Dad stroked her from head to tail in such a deliberate and tender way.

I did not understand why the light dimmed more than usual until another miraculous thing occurred. We could still see the butterflies, but they were joined by what Dad called fireflies. They flew around and would periodically light up. There were so many of them that as they glowed it seemed that they were in perfect harmony. One group would light as the others glow went dark.

Dad smiled and nodded his head. "We called them lightning bugs when we were children. Sometimes the entire backyard was filled with lights flashing on and off. We chased them as kids and even caught some in glass jars. We would turn them loose of course. I don't know why we wanted to catch them. It was just something kids did. I haven't seen any in so long that I can't recall." He smiled contently and whispered, "How beautiful."

We sat quietly—marveling at the miracles of God. Later, the sky grew lighter and the butterflies and the fireflies flew away—replaced once again by the superb colors of evening. I laid my head on top of Sydny, and Dad began to rub us both.

I am just a simple dog that was once discarded by a dumpster. I had no value to those people who I don't recall. But I have gone from a dog that was once deemed as no better than garbage to drawing the attention of God. He left the decision to Cole's mom, but he suggested that I be allowed to greet Dad first. I think he does that all of the time for people on the other side. He whispers suggestions to them but ultimately it is their decision whether to follow his voice. I know this. He desires that all would heed his call but sadly that is not the case. I wondered if people drew a glimpse of this place and what could be their final destination if it would change things, or more importantly, change hearts and minds.

I guess I should be proud that so many people know my story. A dog that refused to seek another place of comfort to live in exchange for living on a hill and keeping *A Watch Over the Gate*. There is so much here that I have not seen. I often refused walks in the woods because I feared even with the trumpet sound—I would not be able to view the gate in time.

Maybe I should have asked permission before I charged past everyone to see my master. But it never crossed my mind. I saw him and nothing could stop me. He laughed when he first saw me and knelt to the ground where I pretty much tackled him. That must be the true expression of love in his life. Sydney once told me that the first time that Dad told Ava that he loved her that he was sitting on the couch facing her. She tackled him and gleefully asked, "Did you just say you love me?" But she knew what she had heard and then she smothered him in kisses and kept repeating, "I love you, Cole Banks. I love you, Cole Banks."

Now I was not there but I bet you anything that Dad just smiled as she kept repeating those words. I will certainly be glad to have her here with us. As I watched Dad—Sydney lying in his lap and being petted once again within an inch of his very life. I know that he will be as I once was. Heaven will be great but not complete until his Ava arrives.

David walked up the hill toward us. Dad rose to meet him. They embraced each other warmly.

"David, I look forward to having time together that we did not have on the other side. You impacted me much despite our limited time spent together."

"I look forward to our time here together as well." He paused before adding, "There is a place across from me that you can have your home built. It is right on the ocean. I know how much you love the water. Even more than me," and then he chuckled. "Maybe more than Jesus and you know our Lord loves the water."

"You once said that to me, didn't you?"

"I believe that I did."

"How did you cope with being in this wonderful place before Sara arrived?"

"By doing as I have done on both sides of the veil. Trusting my Savior."

There was silence before Dad paused and deliberated briefly. "Do you think Dad would allow our home to be built on this hill that my two dogs have waited for me so patiently on? And by Dad, I mean our Father."

"I knew that," he said as he smiled. "I am sure that will be fine.

We just have to get you a building permit."

Dad looked at him quizzically and then David laughed heartily. "Our Father will certainly approve this request. It is not like he did not already know your choice. But I am surprised and not much surprises me here. I thought for sure it would be the ocean that you chose."

"I can see it from here. Heck, I can hear it from here. It is not like I need to hunt for a parking space at Wrightsville Beach on Memorial Day weekend. I can be by the sea in moments.

"The house does not need to be built right away. I think I would like to lie here with Pete and Syd for several evenings."

"I understand."

There was silence again. That is another great thing about this place. No one tries to outtalk each other and when people talk others actually pay attention instead of forming the next words they want to speak in their mind. I think a lot could be solved on the other side if people just really listened to one another.

"I counted the first twenty-one evenings. I know I shouldn't do that, so I stopped." Cole said. "But by now I suspect that they have had my private funeral at the ranch. My ashes have probably been scattered at Carolina Beach where we were married and at Stone Mountain State Park in North Carolina. That is where we honeymooned and where I took Cody when he was little." He paused before adding, "She often asked me not to go where she could not follow."

"Trust," David said, before adding, "I am going into the village." He walked a few steps before he turned back. He had the most amused look on his face. "I understand that you met Johnny Cash."

Cole nodded sheepishly.

And then David burst out laughing. He began walking away again—his final words trailing behind him. "Only you would make a request to hear "Sunday Morning Coming Down," in Heaven. Only you, Cole Banks."

21 ~ David

I heard the whisper and moments later I approached the throne.

"How is Cole adjusting?"

"You know the answers to everything, Lord."

"But I like to hear what you have to say, my dear servant."

"He is concerned about Ava."

"As I am. She sits in that same chair on their porch where Cole sat in the last weeks of his life. She wears his barn coat and drinks coffee from the mug that she did not get to serve him with one last time. She is not riding horses. Those that love her are doing their best but sometimes when I unite and bless something it is as if there is one heartbeat that serves both people."

God smiled generously. "Cole always looked to you as his spiritual father. It is good for you two to have unlimited time together."

"Thank you, Lord." I departed for home.

22 ~ Petra

We were in one of the many creeks across from David's home. Dad was paddling in a nice easy rhythm. We had been kayaking several times. Sydney and I already love it. A large fish jumped and Sydney barked furiously. Oh, this little dog is feisty.

We still rested on the hill in the evenings, and Dad has not mentioned starting to build the home we will all live in together forever. Perhaps there was a problem with the building inspector. It didn't matter to me. I did not require a house in Heaven for my joy to be complete. I was with my dad and that was all that I needed. But for Dad, much like it was for me it will not prove complete until Ava walks through the gate. I noticed that when the trumpet sounds, he always peers intently with a slight hope on his face that he tries to hide. But I see it. I don't know for sure how long it has been since Dad arrived. Of course that is by design. I know Dad had hoped initially that she would soon join him.

Dolphins circled our kayak and one leaped right over our heads. Dad just laughed and all of a sudden, I noticed Sydney's German Shepherd ears perk to full alert.

Sydney barked and Dad seized paddling. Sydney looked off in the distance and barked all the more furiously.

I heard the faint sound of a female voice singing in the distance, but I did not understand why Sydney would bark at that. We heard singing all the time.

> You call me out upon the waters
> The great unknown where feet may fail
> And there I find You in the mystery
> In oceans deep
> My faith will stand
> And I will call upon Your name
> And keep my eyes above the waves

When oceans rise
My soul will rest in Your embrace
For I am Yours and You are mine

Dad smiled and said, "Ava use to sing that when she was part of the worship team at Myrtle Grove. One Sunday after the service this lady Charlotte said, "I could have listened to Ava sing "Oceans," for an hour." Dad chuckled at the thought.

The singing continued, though it was still faint—it seemed to be growing ever so slightly in volume.

Your grace abounds in deepest waters
Your sovereign hand
Will be my guide
Where feet may fail and fear surrounds me
You've never failed and You won't start now
So I will call upon Your name
And keep my eyes above the waves
When oceans rise
My soul will rest in Your embrace
For I am Yours and You are mine

Sydny continued barking and this time he turned to us and said out loud. That is correct. I said out loud. No thoughts being verbalized but the real sound of a mixed breed Chihuahua dog.

"Mom! That is Mom!" He jumped off the kayak and swam to the shore and begin to work his way through the marsh grass. Dad and I jumped off and followed him. We caught up with Sydny, and Dad called out, "Sydny. Stop."

Sydny did as commanded, though I could tell that he was perturbed.

"How do you know?" Dad asked. "Maybe we just want it to be her so badly that it is someone that sounds like her. It's too soon."

"Dad, earth or Heaven—my ears are more sensitive than yours. That is Mom," he stated, leaving no room for doubt.

Dad looked puzzled and I knew he wanted to believe it was so. The voice grew louder.

Spirit lead me where my trust is without borders

Let me walk upon the waters
Wherever You would call me
Take me deeper than my feet could ever wander
And my faith will be made stronger
In the presence of my Savior

Dad's eyes widened, and he took off running. He began to shout, "That is Ava," repeatedly. Sydney turned to me and said, "Didn't I just say that?"

Believe it or not even with four legs we could not keep up with Dad. We were at the bottom of the hill when we saw the most beautiful woman I have ever witnessed in Heaven or on earth.

She was standing still at the top just inside the gates and she continued to sing as Dad made his way to her.

Oh, Jesus, you're my God!
I will call upon Your name
Keep my eyes above the waves
My soul will rest in Your embrace
I am Yours and You are mine

She was belting out the last note. Her voice so powerful—so magnificent that it filled all of Heaven. Dad had made his way to her now. He dropped to his knees and wrapped his arms around her waist. She held his head as if he were the most delicate treasure. Sydney and I had finally reached them. Sydney is jumping on her leg and barking as if he will never cease. I hear laughter all around us.

She stopped singing, and Dad stood and picked her up off her feet. She kissed him and then she grinned at me and said, "Petey, girl. How glad I am to meet you. You will call me Mom," and my heart melted.

Dad twirled her around several times as their laughter filled all of the Heavens. Finally, he placed her down. The four of us begin to walk down the hill. Ava held the hand of the love of her life both before and now here for all eternity. Sydney insisted that she hold him with her free hand.

Dad turned to her and said, "How?"

She smiled and said, "I sat in your chair after Cody and I returned from Stone Mountain to spread your ashes. I prayed without ceasing. I told Jesus that I desired to be with my husband and that my heart would not work without you and then I felt this incredible warmth and I watched as my spirit left my body behind in that chair."

The four of us continued to walk down the hill together. Sydny was barking the entire time. What sheer happiness.

And everyone in Heaven applauded—including God and all the angels.

SONG CREDIT

"Oceans (Where Feet May Fail)" is a song by Australian worship group Hillsong United. The song is led by Taya Smith, and was written by Matt Crocker, Joel Houston and Salomon Ligthelm.